F*CK YOUR EGO

HOW TO APPRECIATE EACH MOMENT, SWITCH OFF AUTOPILOT AND QUESTION REALITY ITSELF.

Ben Cole-Edwards

First published 2020
by Rowanvale Books Ltd
The Gate
Keppoch Street
Roath
Cardiff
CF24 3JW
www.rowanvalebooks.com

A CIP catalogue record for this book is available from the British Library.
Paperback ISBN: 978-1-913662-99-8
ebookISBN: 978-1-914422-00-3

This book is dedicated to my father, Mark.

x

THAT WHICH YOU TRULY BELIEVE IS TRUE, IS TRUE.

INTRODUCTION

So, the baby is finally asleep. I now have anywhere between one minute and three hours to start this book before she wakes.

Where do I even begin? Who am I? What am I? What do I do? I guess the answers to those questions alter the deeper I dive into my own spiritual journey.

It is currently 10:49 a.m. on Saturday the 21st of August, 2021. My latest book, *Retired At 25: The Law of Attraction*, will be published and available across the globe in ten days' time, and since writing that book, I have become a completely different being altogether. I've grown and learned so much about myself, the world, the Universe, time and life itself. *'But Ben, you're only 26—you've barely left school!'* I hear you say. Well, we'll explore the concept of time very soon and then you'll begin to understand why your age, a literal number that simply states how many times you've orbited the sun, has very little bearing on your life.

The title of this book came to me a while after I'd finished writing it. *F*ck Your Ego*. Writing this book taught me a lot about myself but also made me realise that the underlying theme with most of our human problems is the ego itself. Once we learn what our ego is, what it does and how it very rarely serves us, we can then begin to slowly remove it from our lives.

Where are my manners? Hello, hi, buenos días (I'm learning Spanish). I'm Ben Cole-Edwards. Before we go any further, let me first thank you from the bottom of my heart for picking up a copy of this book. I am blessed, grateful and honoured to know that my words have reached you, and I sincerely hope that this book helps you to learn, achieve and receive all that you desire. As I begin to write this book, I've got no plan whatsoever. I guess I'm writing to get all of my teachings on paper. By 'teachings', I simply mean the lessons that I've learned, the theories I've developed and everything that the Universe has channelled through me that may benefit you. The first draft will probably end up as random idea after random idea, but I'll try my best to make it flow in a way that'll expand your knowledge and conscious awareness more and more as you continue to read.

Firstly, though, let's talk about the beginning of *my* journey. I'm going to keep this very brief because if you've read *Retired At 25,* I don't want you to read the same story twice!

I'm from a small town called Maesteg in South Wales, with a population of just over 20,000. The majority of its residents work factory jobs and, I'd like to believe, are very friendly people. It would be deemed weird to walk past someone on the street and *not* say hello and/or mention the weather. My family are all factory workers and come from a rather poor background. My mother and father split when I was two; my mother lost our house and we ended up living in a hostel. I did relatively well in school, was appointed as deputy head boy and was the first in my family to attend university, where I studied acting. After just over a year of ballet and trying to sing, I quit and then made my family extremely proud by getting a job in... you guessed it, a factory. I was loading and unloading scorching hot lorries full of televisions all day for £5.13 an hour. My family were so happy for me and said it was a 'job for life', which I thought was bizarre! I guess it's a generational thing because just a few days ago, actually—even though I never have to work again in my life and can literally buy whatever I want—my grandmother told me about a job vacancy in our town. Best interests at heart and all that.

After around eight months, I decided that I wanted to move on to bigger and better things. I handed in my notice at the factory and took a temporary job at... another factory. No, seriously. I must've bounced between eight to ten factory and office jobs before I stopped working altogether. Just before I discovered the Law of Attraction and the Universe delivered my first big manifestations, I was self-employed as a personal trainer and a massage therapist whilst also working in a supermarket!

2020 was without a doubt the best *and* worst year of my entire life. Again, I won't go into too much detail as I've done that in another book and this isn't X Factor, so you don't need to hear my sob story to like me. In January, like I said, I was working three jobs and had around £200 in the bank. On Friday the 13th of March, I found my grandfather dead. A few months later, my fiancée, Jess, became pregnant after we'd been trying for a while, and then, not long after, on Friday the 21st of August, my father had a heart attack and died, aged 44. In November, my Law of Attraction journey really began, and from then until April 2021, I worked with the Universe to manifest £1.4m, along with a lot of other things, without lifting a finger. Talk about chaos and order.

So, enough about me. I'm guessing you picked this book up because you want to work on your mindset, your outlook on life, and appreciate every conscious moment that you can, right? Fantastic, you're better than your old self already and are sprinting down the right path. Throughout this book, I'm going to be teaching a lot of lessons. I want to transform your perception of reality and life in general and also show you how you can harness the Universal power that is already flowing through you, allowing you to become the ultimate version of YOU.

Let's dive right in, and I want to start with something I've just mentioned. It's something that we all *think* we're familiar with: time.

'WE CRAVE EXPERIENCES THAT WILL MAKE US BE PRESENT, BUT THE CRAVINGS THEMSELVES TAKE US FROM THE PRESENT.'

—Naval Ravikant

TIME

Depending on how distracted you are in this exact moment, this sentence will take you around six seconds to read. But, and excuse my French here, what the fuck is a second!? A second is a fraction of the day, right? And a day is 24 hours? But... what is an hour? Oh, so the Earth spins a full 360° and that takes 24 hours and we call that a day? Cool. So a year, then, is when the Earth orbits around the sun? Right, I understand now.

You see, this is what ruins our perception of time and prevents us from living in each moment as they pass. What you've never questioned before is time itself. Until we break free from this concept, we're slaves to time and therefore live our entire lives by its rules. I know this opening paragraph here kinda makes me seem like I've got a screw loose as I weirdly state the obvious, but let me break it down and hopefully blow your mind.

Your age, let's talk about your age. How 'old' are you? Let's say you're 30. Do you know what that means? You are '30 years old' because, and only because, you have gone around the sun 30 times. That's it. You are factually only 30 years of age because the literal rock that you stand on has travelled around a burning star 30 times, no other reason. 'Oh no, I'm 50 years old! I'm halfway to 100, I'm so old!!' No, no—what you really mean is that you've circled the... you get my point. Einstein, the main man himself, said that time is relative, and without going too deep just yet, you'll soon learn that this current life you're experiencing is the only plane where time actually exists, too.

Now, it's 'time' to explore that a little further. As human beings, we created time, so these rules that we follow aren't set in stone as such, because we literally made them up. Of course, the Earth does take a year to orbit the Sun and 24 hours to spin 360° on its axis, but the way we've labelled it all is really what gets to us. What do I mean by that? We've labelled 12 months as a year. So, when we say 'Wow, I passed my driving test ten years ago, that's flown by, it only seems like yesterday!' we act as though life is going way too fast. Don't get me wrong, life is fast, but isn't it the longest thing we'll ever experience? The only reason we feel as though life is going too fast is because we don't appreciate every moment as it passes and are always waiting for the next 'thing'—more on that in the next section.

So, here's where this concept gets interesting. What if we decided to call ten years, one year? We'd then say 'Wow, I passed my driving test a year ago—that doesn't seem like that long ago!' Exactly, because it wasn't; it was just a 'year' ago. Life only feels so fast because of the labels that us humans have placed on time.

Don't get me wrong, time can be great and quite clearly has a tonne of benefits. You start work at nine, have a break at one and then finish at five, fantastic. You have to attend an important meeting on the 30th of next month? Great! Your flight leaves tomorrow at eight? Awesome, thanks a bunch, time! The labels that we put on time were created for us to use, not for us to be used by. Think about daylight saving time—we literally change the time. It should be 1:00 a.m. now, but let's change that back an hour to help us out. Great. Have you ever questioned that? Have you ever questioned any of this? It's about time you do.

Even though what I'm saying here can sound like a bit of a conspiracy theory, I can assure you it is not. The schedule of the solar system is what it's all based on, and that's all accurate, isn't it? What happens when Elon Musk takes us to Mars and a year there is nearly double a year here? I don't want to get too scientific here, but there's a certain distance from a black hole (very close to it) where you could stay for, say, an hour (provided you're in a rocket with thrusters firing away from the black hole itself to prevent you getting sucked in), and years would have passed back on Earth, due to the way gravity works around a black hole. Have you seen the film Interstellar? You'd return to Earth and, depending on the size of the black hole, one year to millions of years may have passed. How does time work then?

Here's how you can see that time doesn't really exist in your own life. Do you know someone that you'd label as 'old' but they act really young or childish? Do you know a child that speaks like a 60 year old? What makes us grow as individuals is life experience, not hours, days, months or years. My personal perception of life has always been a little different to everyone my own age and I've always had a spiritual mindset, even before 'officially' starting my spiritual journey. I also know people in their seventies and all they do is gossip and look out of the window to see which neighbours are doing what. I'm guessing you know people like that too. You'll chat with them and they'll say things like: 'Oh, Jackie across the road has had new windows. The old ones were disgusting and the new ones aren't much better,' or 'There's a man who works down the shop, and he has really bad breath, but he probably doesn't care about it since his wife left him.' They always want to know what's going on in everyone else's life (normally just the bad things), just so they can reaffirm to themselves that they are superior in every way possible. This is mainly due to the fact that the person has been taken over almost completely by their own ego, which we'll dive into later, but do you know what that gossiping kind of behaviour is called? Childish. So, ask yourself, how can someone have 70 years of life experience but still be a 16 year old on the inside? Because the way we've previously viewed time is false, and you don't necessarily mature with age. How can one person live the same day over and over again until they retire and then get labelled as having 'life experience'? My fiancée's little brother has a friend who's around 12 years old, and if you hear him speak and the things he speaks about, you'd swear he was in his fifties.

Okay, Ben, you've got a point there. But what does this mean for me? How does this affect me? Understanding this concept allows you to start living freely, bound by no walls and governed by no strange laws. Your age does not define you. You can now start to wake up and understand that it is what you do that defines you, not how many candles you have on your birthday cake! Oh, I can't do that, I'm too old! But does it bring you joy? Then do it! The mind is extremely powerful, so when someone tells you 50 years of age is old, you'll immediately feel old on your 50th birthday, because you believed in that person's assumption. We recently met a family on holiday in Kos, Greece, and after I, for some reason, went into great depth about my life and the Law of Attraction with the mother of the family, I started to see the emotional pain that she carried with her, which was 110% due to her perception of age. She told me that she worked in an office and always had, but she was a DJ on the side. She explained how she'd love to DJ more, even full-time, as she was a 'sun-lover' and it was her dream to DJ in various countries. And what was stopping her? Yes, her age. She must've been in her late forties (If you're the lady I'm talking about and reading this and you're like 30, my bad) and she admitted that that was the one thing stopping her. Certain things are associated with certain ages, but why? Take Lego, for example. I fucking love building Lego, and any man that says they don't is either a liar or under the spell of 'time'. You want to know why your husband loves putting Ikea furniture together? It's adult Lego. Anyway, I digress…

When speaking to the woman in Greece, the life coach in me came out and I knew that to massively impact her life, all I had to do was plant the seed. I told her what I've just told you, that age has very little meaning and you definitely do not have to be controlled by it. Imagine if she looked at it the way Sia did? The music was the important part for her, not age, not 'starting late'. Colonel Sanders founded KFC at 62!

Time, my friends, is relative. You always have time on your side, because it is what you make it. This takes me nicely to the next section. If this fake concept of time has now sunk in, how can you unlearn it and live a true life that doesn't fly by?

‘BE WHERE YOU ARE, OTHERWISE YOU WILL MISS YOUR LIFE.’

—Buddha

APPRECIATION

One of the first books I can remember reading that had a serious effect on me and, I'll admit, potentially changed my life, was *The Power of Now* by Eckhart Tolle. I'd like to say I've *always* appreciated everything in life, but I'd be lying. That was until I read his book. Tolle teaches his readers, and definitely taught me, how to *truly* be in the present. In his book, Tolle had me lying down whilst reading and moving my awareness, my energy, around my body. I'd recommend getting a copy to experience it for yourself, but here's the essence of one of my favourite lessons. This is also a great way to start a meditation and to 'ground' yourself.

Whilst in a comfortable position and really focusing on your breathing, place your inner awareness in your feet. Really feel your awareness and energy there. When done right, it'll feel like a weight in your feet. Give it a go now, if you'd like. After 30 seconds or so, move that awareness, also known as inner chi, up your body and through every limb. Once you've experienced being *in* every body part, you'll come to your head. What this technique does is centres you and allows you to be fully *in the moment*. No thoughts, no stress, no worry, just you in the moment. What really—and I mean really—baffled me was when I was introduced to what a 'moment' actually was. So, here's my take.

Please, take in every word here. All you <u>ever</u> have is this *exact* moment. Once you realise that you're in this one moment, and I mean literally right this second as you read these words, and this moment is all you have and all that's guaranteed, everything changes. There is no past and there is no future. I've spoken about the concept of time, so putting that and this together means that the 'future' is just one moment at another time. Something that you've done in the past, then, was just a single moment at another time. Once you truly understand this one moment that you're in, you'll *really* begin to feel like you're in your body and not just living on autopilot. You'll also take in more of your surroundings, like you've never used your peripherals before. You'll see more colours and things will appear brighter. Do it now—look up from this page now and take in your surroundings. This is <u>all</u> you have.

Each moment as it passes is all you get, so let's learn to appreciate them, no matter what each moment brings. Stop constantly looking for what I like to call 'attention food'. Stop taking yourself away from the moment that you have by seeking out something that keeps your mind off the 'now'. I do it too, sometimes. I'll be learning Spanish on my phone, then once I'm done, I'll pick up the book I'm reading. Once I'm done reading, I'll choose something to watch on TV, all whilst simultaneously scrolling Twitter. When we do this, we *ignore* the 'now' and live like robots, trying to feed our attention. Change that. Allow your body to just sit and observe, sit and breathe. Take it all in.

There is no good and bad, only a situation and how you view and respond to it. It's not about the circumstances that we face but *how* we choose to face them. I don't mean to get too deep and trigger any emotions here, but have you ever lost someone close to you and it pains you to think about them? After my father died, it hurt my heart to look at photos and videos of him. The fact that he was no longer here, never got the chance to meet my daughter and was going to miss out on so much, just physically hurt. It wasn't until I changed the way I *looked* at this situation that my entire outlook on it changed for the better. Looking back at photos and videos now? Pure happiness. I am so happy and grateful that he was *my* father, that it was *me* who learned those things from him and that he was a part of *my* life. Once you change the way you look at things, the things you look at change.

As I've mentioned, 2020 was very traumatic for me, and I feel as though it rewired my brain. For a long time, I couldn't hear the words 'heart attack', 'drop dead' or 'collapse' without my brain taking me back to a dark place and the flashbacks kicking back in. Now, however, I can see that 2020 taught me the most valuable lessons there are: appreciation and gratitude. You may think that those words mean the same thing, but throughout this book, I hope to change that and give each one a slightly different meaning.

I now appreciate every single moment that I can. And I say 'that I can', because to truly appreciate *every* moment would be a superpower that even a monk would be envious of. This year I have unfollowed everyone on Instagram besides Jess; I unfollowed all but 30 people on Twitter and deleted Facebook from my phone. Social media is bizarre, and if it's good at doing one thing, it's taking our attention from our own lives and onto someone else's. Think about it. The next time you are scrolling through your social feed, ask yourself why. You are feeding your brain with information regarding the lives of other people, subconsciously comparing their lives to yours. Don't forget that it's all a highlight reel too, and note that not everything is posted. Oh, Sarah just posted a photo of her new, flashy car? Did she also mention the £350 per month finance, the £130 per month insurance, the tax, the running costs and how she still lives in her mother's spare room? Give yourself a break. And I'm not some guru here, I've been there and scrolled for hours and hours at every opportunity I had. 2020 made me realise that I wasn't living *in* the moment, and it took becoming a father myself to make me *appreciate* each moment.

The idea with unfollowing everyone on Instagram besides Jess was that if I was on autopilot and subconsciously opened the app up to scroll, I'd only see photos that I'd posted or Jess posted, and 99% of the time it'd be a photo of our daughter, Piper. This would then make my conscious self question my subconscious self, and my inner voice would say '*What are you doing on your phone? You're a father.*' I had discovered how the Universe really works in regard to giving you anything you desire (don't worry, I'll teach you that too), so I am now truly blessed to not have to work, which allows me to spend every day with my daughter.

Appreciation doesn't just have to be about people, though. Being appreciative opens emotional doors that were previously walls, and it also blocks a lot of feelings of negativity.

Let's go back to viewing a situation differently so we can learn how to enhance our daily experiences.

Do you hate your job? It's extremely common for people to not enjoy what they do for work these days.

Same shit, different day, eh? Later on, when I talk about the power of the mind, I'll explain to you how you only hate your job *because* you keep saying you hate your job. But for now, how can you begin to appreciate that job you *don't* love? For me, I *had* to learn to love a job that I dreaded going to, otherwise I was going to quit and that wasn't really a great financial option. Before I took the supermarket job, I was self-employed full-time as a personal trainer. I was also delivering mail in the early hours of the morning, but I never told social media that because I wanted them to believe I was doing so well with personal training alone—highlight reel and all that jazz. So, when I took the supermarket job, my ego took a hit. When I quit university, I wrote a crime/thriller novel and had it published. I barely made a few hundred pounds, but the title of 'author' made people think I'd made it big. One guy that I was in school with came up to me on a night out years ago and told me that I was the most successful person he went to school with. I felt like a fraud, but my ego loved it. The same person approached me in the supermarket and asked why I was working there because he thought I was 'doing well'. My ego didn't like that quite as much. That was one of the reasons why I didn't like the job, also because it was part-time and I applied thinking it was full-time because they'd made a mistake when advertising, which meant that I was constantly begging for overtime. My shifts were usually 5 p.m.–11 p.m., so I'd be waiting around all day and thinking about how much I didn't want to go to work. I had to sell my car (that was £600, £400 of which was borrowed) because I was so short on money, and I'd then walk/cycle ten minutes to work. This meant that I'd have time to think about the negative parts of my life and how I wasn't going anywhere, as I walked home alone in the middle of the night.

Then, I changed the way I was *looking* at it and began to *appreciate* this job that I'd hated so much. But how did I do that? I simply stopped looking at the negatives and started to consistently pick out all the good things. Firstly, I had a job that meant I could put food on the table for my partner and I. Secondly, the job was up the road so I could walk to it, meaning I saved money on transport and also got some fresh air and exercise in. Thirdly, the time I spent going to and from work could either be used to plan things to attract more clients to my personal training business, or just to listen to feel-good music to get me in a good mood. And fourth, I'd attended university and studied acting because I saw myself as the next Jim Carrey and I thrived off making people laugh and being an entertainer. I took this to the supermarket. I decided that I was going to make it my goal each shift to make at least one person laugh. I'd walk in early on a Sunday morning with my earphones blasting (usually Elvis) and bust a move, guaranteed to put a smile on at least one person's face, or at least have my sanity questioned. I'd see colleagues, and even customers, looking down in the dumps and I'd feel as though I *had to* perk them up a little. Each colleague had their own interests and hobbies, so I'd use those things to get them talking and forget about their worries, or forget how much they hated their job, too. Giving is the best state to receive. Someone can be falling apart on the inside and not show it on the outside, so always do your best to share a smile. To love the job even more, as I went further and further along my spiritual path, I learned (and will teach you) how to remove my ego. No outside opinions ever bothered me once I achieved that.

Of course, I'm telling you all this so that you can apply it to your own life. What do you have in your life that you don't like but can't yet change? Is it your car? Do you wish it was prettier? Faster? Newer? But it gets you to work, doesn't it? It gets you to the shops to get food for your children, doesn't it? You can rely on it in case there's an emergency, can't you? Or is it your house? Would you prefer it if you had a garage? If it was in a nicer area? If you had an extension? But there's a roof over your family's head, isn't there? You don't live in a hostel, do you? You have a place to sleep, right? You get my point.

There'll always be something, though, no matter how 'successful' you become. When I bought my first dream car, a Range Rover Sport, after trying to manifest it for a while, I still had in the back of my mind: *'But it isn't a Lamborghini, is it?'* Your ego will always try to win—even mine does, after I've tried my best to remove it. The principle here is simple: the grass always appears greener on the other side, but the grass is truly greener wherever you choose to water it. Begin to water your garden and not the idea of someone else's, and you may even see some flowers grow where there were previously weeds.

Before the next section, I want to quickly touch upon appreciating your pets. I've got two French Bulldogs: Romeo and Cooper. Before becoming 'spiritual' and switching autopilot off whenever I can remember too, I'd sit on the sofa watching TV or scrolling mindlessly on my phone. After a few hours, I'd get bored of refreshing my apps and lock my phone, and then I'd realise that my dogs had been right next to me the whole time, just wanting attention. I read a quote once that said something along the lines of 'A dog may be a part of your life, but to a dog, you are its whole life' and that stuck with me. All your pets have is you. Your pets are living beings with brains and hearts and emotions, so treat them like it. A great way to do this immediately is to imagine that after your days, you arrive in Heaven, or whatever that place is called for you. When you get there, your pets come sprinting towards you, smiling, and you play with them and love them because you've not seen them in years. Imagine how you'd act and respond to their little faces. And act like that now. If you're not a pet person though (weird), ignore this paragraph!

THE UNIVERSE IS NOT OUTSIDE OF YOU. LOOK INSIDE YOURSELF; EVERYTHING THAT YOU WANT, YOU ALREADY ARE.'

—Rumi

EGO

In this book's introduction, I explained how the ego is the underlying theme in most of our problems. In this section, I'm going to talk specifically about the ego and how you can turn its volume down so the only voice you hear is your own, and not the jealous words within that feed on appearing better than everyone else. The old me lived on that line between confident and arrogant, and looking back I can see that 90% of the things I did were to impress other people and to look good. Around the age of 20-21 (what *is* age though?), I had been working out at the gym for around four or five years but was still very skinny. I'd been called skinny throughout my life, but even more so whilst being at university. When I told people that I didn't like it, because I was training and eating a lot, they found it even funnier to call me skinny.

I believe—and I've only realised this since looking back to understand it—that the reason I was never happy skinny was because on holiday once there was this guy in great shape, and my mother told me that if I did 500 push-ups and sit-ups each night, I could look like that. I think that lit a spark in 14-year-old me's brain that told me that *that* was what I should look like. Anyway, after training (which I was doing wrong) and dieting (which I wasn't doing right either) and getting minimal results, I started experimenting with steroids. I started by taking tablets. I remember taking the first one in front of my mother, and I said, with a smile on my face, 'I'm on steroids!' My mother responded with, 'And you're proud of that, are you?' Like, do you want me to be big and muscly or not!

After getting a little bigger and a little stronger, like with everything else in my life, I wanted more. I hated needles, but I started injecting steroids. I just wanted to get bigger and fill my T-shirts and for girls to fancy me. How bizarre is that? At the time I thought I was just getting ahead. I found it strange that my friends were training *without* steroids, oblivious to what it was doing to my physical and mental health. I also found that it heightened my emotions. If I was happy, I was ecstatic and if I was sad, I was depressed. Even when I started my personal training business, I felt as though the bigger and better 'in shape' I was, the more clients I would take on. This wasn't the case, however, because I stopped taking everything altogether when Jess and I started trying for a baby, and then I took on more clients than ever, at my skinniest in years! Now, at 26, I don't train whatsoever. I go to the beach and paddleboard most mornings when the weather is decent, but that's about as far as my fitness goes these days, and that's by choice. I feel great with the body I now have, it's as simple as that.

If you're reading this and are unhappy with the way you look, take a look at the people you follow on social media. Everything is edited these days, so all those 'in shape' people only look that way because of lighting, angles and Photoshop. The way your body is and the shape you're in *is* the way that you're supposed to look. If you're unhealthy or want to look different for *you,* then that's fair enough. Just make sure you're not putting those hours in at the gym to impress someone else or to 'fit in'.

Jay Shetty puts it best in his book *Think Like a Monk*, where he mentions the following quote, which will blow your mind:

'I'm not what I think I am, I'm not what you think I am, I am what I think you think I am.'

Please read that until it makes sense and sinks in. It teaches us that we're caught not in a perception of ourselves, but in a perception of a perception.

Allow me to apply the quote to my own life for it to make more sense. Back when I was on steroids, I got to the point where I would only really take them around eight weeks before a holiday, simply to look better in photos by the pool. You see, I was only trying to keep up this 'image' of myself for social media. In my head, everyone *knew* I was in shape and the first thing they thought of when thinking about me was the shape I was in. Therefore, I felt the *need* to train and take enhancement drugs to live up to their idea of me. The thing is, no one really thought of my body when my name was mentioned. They just thought of Ben, just me.

So, let's go back to the quote and break it down. 'I'm not what *I* think I am.' I wasn't trying to look good to reassure myself or even reaffirm to my own mind who and what I was. 'I'm not what *you* think I am.' I thought I was aiming to look better for my social media 'audience' as it were, but they thought of me as Ben, the person, and not just someone with a six-pack. 'I am what I *think* you think I am.' I tried my hardest to get good photos whilst topless on holidays, just to live up to the expectations I *thought* other people had of me, which were false, after all.

Is this making your eyes widen? Can you relate it to your own life? Have you ever made a fancy new purchase, maybe a designer bag, shoes or even a car? What was your reasoning behind it? Did you buy it because you liked it, or was the underlying motive the fact that you *thought* that people thought you had a lot of money, so you felt as though you had to live up to that false perception? I know I have. When I came out of uni, I took out a £10,000 loan and blew it in three weeks. I bought a car, spent money on the car, got tattoos and went on holiday. It was a stupid thing to do and very reckless, but at the age of 19, £10,000 felt like £1,000,000 (even though I spent it like it was £5). After blowing the bank's money and having to pay £259 each month for five years, I posted a photo on Instagram, which was again to satisfy my ego and *be* someone else's perception, which didn't even exist. I uploaded a photo of Leonardo DiCaprio in the film *The Wolf of Wall Street* where he's throwing money off of his yacht and calling the money 'fun coupons'. I captioned it with something along the lines of 'If you think you're bad with money, I just blew £10,000 in three weeks!' I posted it with a huge grin on my face, hoping that all my followers would now see how well I was doing. Did I tell them about the factory job I was working at where I was also getting bullied daily? Absolutely fucking not.

Old cartoons have always depicted the angel on one shoulder and the devil on another. For me, that 'devil' is your ego. Your ego thrives off knowing that you are superior to everyone else. On the flip side, however, if you do something against your ego—for example, if you have a bad haircut when you care a lot about your appearance—then your ego will make you feel like you're the size of an ant. Your ego will battle with the egos of others too. If, like old me, you're insecure about a certain body part (I always had small calves and could never get them to grow) and that's something people know about, their egos will make them mention it, to hurt your ego. I had morbidly obese people make comments about how thin my legs were, and you could tell by their faces that they loved pointing it out.

So, Ben, you said you 'removed' your ego. How is that possible? Well, at the end of the day, if you don't want to listen to someone speak, tell them to shut up. The ego is simply a nasty little voice inside filled with hate. I've 'removed' my ego, but it still creeps up on me sometimes. I'll be driving through town with the windows down, playing Kanye West, and I'll see loads of people turn their heads to look at the car. That feeds my ego. I also give a lot of money to charity, and I'm a sucker for donating to people who need money for their dogs' operations. As I've mentioned, giving is the best state to be in in order to receive. That being said, of course, it makes my ego feel good to give other people money because it reminds me of the abundance that I have. Even typing that stroked my ego a little. You just need to know when to listen to it and when to lock it up and throw away the key.

My mother was a nightmare for fighting with my ego. To this day, she still isn't happy with her body and wants to diet better, train better and even get surgery. Without her conscious knowledge, the fact that she was always unhappy with her body made her ego criticise mine. I was taking steroids and looking better and better each week, and she'd make a comment about me having skinny legs or mention the fact that I'd 'never be big' because I'm 'not built that way' (which only made my ego try to convince me to take *more* steroids). When my mother met Jess, she (her ego) would 'joke' about how Jess should make comments about me being skinny because 'he doesn't like that haha'. I've not lifted a single weight for almost a year now, and recently my mother said, 'You could do with putting on some weight.' I really had her stumped, speechless even, when I asked 'Why?' She had no answer. I mean, what could be the possible benefit of me being 'bigger'? I'd have to go back to eating seven meals a day, which was not only torture but very expensive. Let's also say that I went back to the gym five days a week. That's two hours a day away from home, which means I'd be spending forty hours a month away from my daughter. No chance. Don't get me wrong, I'm still in decent shape (that's my ego speaking, not me) but getting bigger, for me, simply isn't natural. Even my grandparents questioned whether I was eating or not because I'd lost a lot of weight. Like, yeah, you've just gotten used to me being almost quite literally addicted to drugs. Health is wealth.

Yeah, that's great and all, but how do I quieten my ego? The answer to that is all about the strength of a question. Let's talk about that.

‘ENLIGHTENMENT IS THE SPACE BETWEEN YOUR THOUGHTS.’
—Eckhart Tolle

QUESTION

In his book *Awaken the Giant Within*, Tony Robbins talks about the power of a question, and I know I keep saying this, but this concept also 'changed my life', which is why I'm sharing it. Using the power of certain questions has stopped me from thinking negative thoughts altogether, got me out of bad moods and even allowed me to give myself the answers that I'd previously been looking for externally. It sounds so simple to do but really does have such a profound effect on your mental health, mood and wellbeing.

Okay, so, the next time you're feeling *any* emotion besides joy, ask yourself *why* you are feeling that way. Like I said, sounds easy, right? Trust me, once you do this it'll feel like a breath of fresh air whenever you may be falling off track.

I'm first going to use myself as an example again here. When I made my first £100,000, I felt filthy rich. Within a week I'd made another £130,0000 and a few days later I was back down to £100,000, and boy was I depressed. I'd turned £6700 into £230,000 in a few weeks via the stock market (later on I'll tell you how I know nothing about the stock market and how this was all down to manifestations, affirmations and the Law of Attraction) and then lost £130,000 in a few days after only just making it. I now had £100,000 and felt poor, like I had nothing at all. I could feel the hairs on my head turning grey, and it felt like I didn't put my phone down for a whole week as I continued to watch my portfolio plummet. I was seriously down. You're probably thinking: 'Grow up, you had six figures, that's mega money!' I felt the same way when I first hit that milestone, but not after I lost loads and came back down to the same figure. But then I took Tony Robbins' advice and asked myself *why* I was feeling so sad. I mean, you're right, I had a lot of money, so I told myself that. My inner monologue went something like this:

'I'm so broke. What am I going to do?'

'You literally had £6700 like three weeks ago.'

'Yeah, I know, but—'

'And £200 a few months before.'

'Yeah, that's true, but I lost a lot of mon—'

'Was it in the bank?'

'Well, not technically.'

'And how long was your portfolio at £230,000?'

'Like, two minutes.'

'Then shut up.'

I had to get in my own head and question my feelings and, more specifically, *why* I was feeling that way before I could feel anything else.

Now, I know that that *exact* story doesn't relate to everyone, but the idea behind it does and I use this technique very often. I recently used this technique with my grandmother. She was upset because it was coming up to the one-year anniversary of my father's passing. First, I introduced her to what a 'year' actually was and why it had no meaning, and secondly, I explained my belief that if you miss someone, you miss them regardless of 'time'. Sure, a date in the calendar reminds you of someone's passing, but it should have no significance on your emotions.

Jess's mother acts in the exact same way. Before moving into our own house, I lived with Jess' family for just over a year. One day, when it was only Jess's mother and me at home, I noticed her quietly crying to herself whilst in the kitchen. I asked her what was wrong and she explained that it was the anniversary of her mother's passing. She told me that she cries on the same date every year, but it's usually just her home alone, so no one knew. I hadn't consciously begun my spiritual journey back then, so I saw her reasoning, agreed with her and tried my best to comfort and reassure her. Now, however, especially after losing people myself, I can see that this reaction is simply a trick that your brain plays on you, making you upset over nothing more than another orbit around the sun. Once you truly question your thoughts and emotions, you get to decide and hand-pick, as it were, what you want to choose to feel. No one controls your emotions but you.

Have you ever gone through a break-up and felt completely miserable afterwards? Like your entire world had crumbled before you? I bet you never got to the root of that feeling, though, did you? You felt as though that person was your 'other half', which then made you incomplete without them, and you left it at that. You just gave up on the reasons and started to focus solely on the emotion, letting it take over you and control you every day. *But I loved that person.* Did you? Or did you love the *idea* of them? Question that. Were there things in that relationship that you didn't like, that didn't work, but you overlooked them because you were blinded by what you thought was love? I'm a firm believer in the idea that every single thing happens for a reason, so if that person was 'the one' for you, then you'd still be with them. What if you were now to consider the positives of the situation? You're newly single, as young as you feel and quite literally have the Universe at your fingertips. You no longer have ties, you can go wherever you like in the world, do whatever you want and, more importantly, *be* whoever you want to be. Doesn't sound all that bad now, does it?

We can tie this in with the appreciation of a job you hate, too. If you hate your job or dislike a certain person there, ask yourself why. For me, the reason why I hated my job was because of my ego, and once I understood that and came to terms with it, I could learn to solve the issue and love my job. Think of someone you dislike. I'm going to be cliché and say it's your boss. Why do you dislike them so much? Go on, ask yourself the question. Do you envy your boss because they earn more money than you? Do you think you could do their job but have never been given the opportunity? Is it an authority problem that your ego has, which makes you feel belittled when your boss tells you to do something? That's their job, at the end of the day. Now, if any of those reasons are true for you, reverse them. Can you feel happy for your boss, knowing that they have the salary to give their kids a great life? Can it motivate you to create your own opportunities to be in the same position? The next time you get told to do something, can you do it better and faster than before, allowing your boss to really see your potential and offer you a promotion when one arises? All it takes is one question, so don't be afraid to ask yourself a few. What's the worst that can happen? You'll ignore yourself?

'WORRYING IS USING YOUR IMAGINATION TO CREATE SOMETHING YOU DON'T WANT.'
—Esther Hicks

GRATITUDE

Towards the start of this book, I mentioned how appreciation and gratitude mean different things. This is all to do with manifesting using the Law of Attraction. You can be grateful for things that you desire but don't yet have, thus attracting those things into your life.

In this section, though, we're going to practice gratitude, and even *realise* our gratitude, for things we have in our lives already.

First, the obvious. There are millions and millions of people living what you and I wouldn't even consider a 'life'. Some are on the streets, some have no clean water and some feel as though they have no free will. Don't you find it crazy that we use clean, fresh water to wash our dishes, but some people don't have clean water to drink? What about how we complain that our homes aren't big enough or in a nice enough area, but there are people living in huts made of mud? The morals of the world are so twisted. Imagine if we utilised the billions we spend on wars and instead spent the money where it's *actually* needed. At the end of the day, money will almost always solve the problems that I'm talking about, and money is just pieces of paper and numbers in the bank. Something that, again, humans have created for us to use and instead, it uses and controls us. Some are chained to debt by this invisible idea of finances, and some can't live half a decent life because they don't have enough of this paper. I've gone off on a passionate tangent here, but you get my point.

What do you have in your life that you really do take for granted? It's probably an extensive list, never-ending almost. The perfect time to list the things you're grateful for is just before you go to sleep and just after you wake up, which are crucial times. You see, at these times, your brain is in a different state and operates on different wavelengths, and this state makes your brain more susceptible to new information. If you wake up and think thoughts of gratitude, that'll have a massive impact on the way you view the rest of your day, and you'll almost always be more grateful for your encounters that day.

Dr Joe Dispenza, someone who combines science with spirituality and teaches people how to heal diseases using meditation and their mind alone, talks about this morning routine a lot. So, what's the first thing you normally do as soon as you wake up? 90% of you are going to say it's checking your phone, aren't you? Before your eyes even adjust to the morning sunlight, you're checking your notifications and having a cheeky scroll, am I right? But—back to questioning everything—do you know why you do that? I was a sucker for it too, so believe me when I say it's a bad habit. Dangerous, even. You check your phone to reaffirm to your brain, ego and self *who* you actually are and to confirm that the world you went to sleep in is still the same world that you've woken up to. If you believe that the world has gone mad and that there's always a news story about a murder or crime or an attack, then your brain wants you to check Facebook to hopefully find another similar story just so it can confirm to yesterday's you that the world is the same place as the day before.

You'll scroll through all your feeds, check your emails, look to see if you've received any new likes on your latest upload, any retweets on Twitter, etc., etc. You're only doing this, like with the news stories, to reconfirm who *you* are, and to make sure it's the same person you were yesterday. Do you normally get 100 likes on each photo you upload? You'll check for that in the morning. *Another hundred likes—phew, I'm still loved.* You may also check your WhatsApp or the group chat messages to reassure yourself that you still have people to call friends.

This also works in the opposite way. If you're in a bad way emotionally, feel as though you have no one to speak to and no one to turn to, you'll also check your socials in the morning to make sure you've still not received any notifications, which is literally just to keep you in the bad mood that you're in.

I hope by now this has really resonated with you and you've started to identify your own ego and understand that it *isn't* your best friend. Stop feeding it, especially as soon as you wake up in the morning. Here's what to do instead.

Begin by creating a list of five things that you're grateful for. Even I struggled to think of five to begin with. My daughter... my family... my finances... my car? It goes soooo much further beyond that, though! You can actually spend hours doing this, if you like, but a minute or two is plenty to begin with. Before you go to bed, really think of what you're grateful for, and start with where you are. Is your pillow nice and soft? Your bed comfy? Your home warm and dry? The street you live on peaceful and quiet at night with no dogs barking in the distance? Did you experience any pain in your body today? Do all your limbs work as they should? Did you smile today? Be grateful for those things. Give thanks for the things that you've never given thanks for before. It'll spark a new-found love for the little things. And as we've always been taught, in all aspects of life, the little things add up. Of course, the things in our immediate surroundings are just some examples of things we all take for granted, so don't forget to write down what you are *truly* grateful for, and by that, I mean the things that are closest to your heart and you value the most. Your family, your health, and you being here to live and seize each day: start there.

'EVERY MAN HAS TWO LIVES, AND THE SECOND ONE BEGINS WHEN HE REALISES HE ONLY HAS ONE.'

—Confucius

JOY

Do well in school, get good grades, get a good job, take out a mortgage, marry, have kids, work for the rest of your fucking life and die. If there's one thing I want you to try out the power of questioning on, it's that. I mean, come on, that is not life and most certainly not how your 'years' should be lived. Get a home and start a family, of course, by all means, but make sure you're happy when doing so.

So, who came up with this? Who engrained this lifelong image into our minds? Was it our parents? Teachers? A bit of both, actually. Yes, your parents and your teachers tell you that there's no other option but to climb the monotonous ladder of life, but your parents only told you that because *their* teachers drilled it into their heads, and their parents' teachers before them. I'm not going to get into how it's actually the government that makes sure that these 'teachings' are implemented throughout school so the rich stay rich and the poor stay poor, but hey ho, the seed is there.

The thing is, throughout my life, I always looked up to teachers. Figures of authority, role models and leaders with the responsibility of enriching the minds of the next generation, right? I'm 100% sure I'll be home-schooling my daughter when the time comes, partly because why would I bring a child into the world just to ship them off to school for six hours a day and not see them, and partly because the majority of things kids are taught in school are never ever used again in their lives other than in exams.

Here's a funny little question though, do you *know* a teacher? Like, personally, outside of them being a teacher? Now I'm not speaking for all teachers out there, but as someone who went to university and had a lot of friends who studied to become (and are now qualified and working as) teachers, the majority of them were (and still are) just party animals who barely attended any actual lectures. A good point to note is that to get a qualification, whether it's a doctorate or a GCSE, you just need to have a good memory. Do you, like I do, know people who smashed all of their school exams out of the park but now work jobs that pay minimum wage? Or someone who failed every test that was given to them but now runs their own successful business? Simply put, that's because a qualification doesn't define someone, and to be quite frank, doesn't mean anything. I know personal trainers who paid thousands for an online course to become qualified to train others, spending months to add 'nutritionist' to their belts, and still have no clients. In the three years that I was a personal trainer myself, I took on over 550 clients and had zero qualifications. What I'm trying to get at here is that just because some normal person with a 'qualification' tells you to study hard to get a job to essentially live to die doesn't mean you have to listen to them.

Ben, you've titled this section 'Joy' but are just hating on schools and calling teachers alcoholics, am I missing something? Sorry, I went off on one again, but here's what I'm trying to say. You need to live the life that you WANT to live. You must live *your* life and not just be a cog in someone else's. When I began to pull myself out of a dark hole last year, I started by picking up three books. I purchased *Just F*cking Do It* by Noor Hibbert, *Think and Grow Rich* by Napoleon Hill and *The Law Of Attraction - The Teachings of Abraham* by Jerry and Esther Hicks. I picked up the first one to learn how I could change my mindset, the second to learn how I could possibly improve my financial situation and the third to obviously just learn about the Law of Attraction. I read them in the order that I've just written them, and when I was around halfway through the second book, it hit me that they were *all* about this 'Law of Attraction'. I took that as a sign that something/someone higher than me really wanted me to learn about it all. It was either that or a big ol' coincidence, but here I am writing my second book since retiring at 25. Spoiler: it works.

I'm telling you this because since reading those three books, I have lost count of how many other books on the topic I have read. Funnily enough, most of them I bought thinking they'd be about something else. What all of these books teach is that the key meaning and sole purpose of this life is to seek **joy**. Find your joy and spread the joy. If you do that, you can't go far wrong.

But what do I mean by 'joy' exactly? As a child, your imagination was wild, wasn't it? You could play pretend with your toys for hours. Then you were told that that was 'childish' and to stop. Then maybe you loved playing video games, but then, at some age, someone told you that you needed to stop because they believed it wasn't 'productive' or 'mature'. If *anyone* has something negative to say about whatever you're doing (which brings you joy, and isn't illegal), that only means they've lost ways to find their own joy, even if their negativity is a subconscious reaction.

So what brings *you* joy? I'm a big Marvel nerd and absolutely love Spider-Man. I've recently started collecting figures and replica props from Hong Kong and displaying them in my bookcase. In the beginning, Jess—a great example here—thought that it was a waste of money and childish that I was 26 and 'playing with toys', but every time I walk past the figures and see my Spider-Man mask (with remote controlled moveable eyes, may I add) especially, it truly brings me joy and puts a big fat smile on my face. Side note, the mask was £20 and not £250 if she asks, thanks. I like playing video games every now and again too, from Spider-Man to GTA to even blowing the cobwebs off of my old Gameboy once in a while to play Pokémon. If you play video games, then you know that it can sometimes act as a distraction, which can be useful. Worrying about something does absolutely nothing for you or the situation and simply means you are feeling negative emotions about a future scenario that hasn't even happened. Video games and similar things can instead let your mind be at ease as you place your focus elsewhere. I'm not condoning 'ignoring' your problems as such, because all issues need to be faced, but finding a joyous thing for you that absorbs you and your negative emotions momentarily can be great for you.

Okay, enough about me being a nerd, it's your turn. I'm just going to reel off a few things here to get your brain rolling. Many people, even though they don't do it as often as they should, find joy in things like football, being outdoors, hiking, martial arts, going for a long drive, being at the beach, swimming in the sea, reading, watching comedy, writing, cooking, painting, listening to music, dancing—the list is obviously never-ending. So where do your joyous activities come in? Keep a few things in your head that you thoroughly enjoy doing and that you know bring you joy. How often do you perform those activities? You love busting a move to music? Great, me too. How frequently do you find yourself in a great mood as you moonwalk across the living room? Is that something you do for 15 minutes a day, once a month, or can you simply not recall the last time you performed that joyous act? I mentioned earlier on in the book how I used to walk into the supermarket for work simultaneously listening to music and spreading my energy and my joy to everyone who looked my way. What I was also doing was spending 30 minutes at home beforehand rocking out to some great songs and jiving in the mirror, raising my frequency to match the version of me that is stress-free and has zero worries. I'll explain frequencies and how to raise yours later on.

So, once you've identified what activities you find joy in, and the lack of time you spend doing those things, bring back that questioning technique that you've been developing so rapidly. Why *aren't* you doing what makes you happy? Why aren't you doing things that you find joy in? Don't have enough time to go to the beach for a late evening stroll? How many episodes of that Netflix series have you watched this week? Ten hours' worth? Twenty? More? Or is the problem money? Did you sell your guitar many years ago, even though you loved strumming away? You know you'd love another one, but you think it's a lack of funds that's stopping you from buying again, right? Check your bank statement and see just how much money you've wasted on fast food or coffee this month, then ask yourself again. We aren't robots and our lives aren't meant to be 'do this', 'do this', 'do this', 'do this'. Does reading, learning and self-development bring you joy? Awesome, keep reading, and I hope you'll learn a thing or two about yourself, if you haven't already. If that's not you, though, and you can think of another activity that you could do right this second that'll bring you happiness and allow you to forget about work in the morning or school or that meeting you're dreading (if you're not yet grateful for those things), then put this book down and get out there and do it! What's the time right now? Too late to go surfing? No problem, what about listening to music? Too stressed to let your mind focus on anything but the issues you think you face? Have you tried meditation? You'll definitely find joy there. There's always something you can do to bring you joy. If all else fails, jump up and dance to music. I know I've mentioned the music and dancing thing several times now, but it's because it's what I find works best. No one else controls your body but you, so tell it to get up and shake what your mama gave ya! Try doing that in a bad mood, I dare you! While we're speaking of you being in control of your body, are you sure your body isn't the one that's really running the show?

'WHATEVER THE MIND CAN CONCEIVE AND BELIEVE, IT CAN ACHIEVE.'
—Napoleon Hill

AUTOPILOT

Throughout my spiritual journey so far, I've found so much contradictory advice in regard to your body and mind. One book/guru teaches that to achieve enlightenment, one needs to merge their body and mind. The next book teaches that your body and mind are separate 'beings', as it were, and another book may teach that your body is but a suit of flesh that our souls are currently occupying. I think they're all right in their own ways, and you'll probably find me contradicting myself in this book along the way too. However, here's an interesting, fresh idea to feast your eyes upon. What if your *body* is the thing that's in charge here, running your day-to-day life and you (the mind) are just the backup program, waiting to kick in if needed?

This is where I like to use the term 'autopilot'. For those of you who know the term and maybe think they know the meaning, this'll be fun. Being on autopilot is self-explanatory, but just in case, it's what we call it when a pilot switches the aeroplane into 'self-drive' mode. Or self-fly mode? We've coined this term for certain parts of our lives, and the most common scenario in which we use it and it's the most relatable is when you're driving down a long road and you get to the end of the road and think, 'Oh shit, I can't remember driving down this road! Was that light even green?' because your mind simply went blank and your *body* did all the work. Whenever that's mentioned, however, everyone laughs it off.

You've heard of muscle memory, right? If you think about it on a consciousness level, however, you'll see that the majority of people spend 99% of their day on autopilot. The other 1% is when they're *thinking* of what to eat for dinner. I used italics for 'thinking' there because that's what gets you out of autopilot: conscious thoughts. We've previously talked about being 'in the moment', which is something I'd deem as crucial for breaking the habit of having autopilot automatically come on, usually from the second you wake up. Unfortunately, and quite sadly, the majority of you can relate to what I'm about to say. Wake up, check phone, pee, rush breakfast, brush teeth, fight traffic, hate work and the people you work with, fight traffic, eat, TV, social media, bed. That was me for almost ten years, and I wish someone had put it so bluntly for me when I first started working full-time. This may open your eyes to your own reality, and it's harsh. It blew my mind once I could see that my entire life had been on autopilot when I thought I'd been the one in control all along.

Okay, back to what I said about your body being in the driver's seat and not you. When I mention 'you' here, I'm referring to your mind. So, if the body is in the driver's seat, are you sitting in the passenger's seat? Nope, not even riding shotgun! The back seat? Nope! In the trunk?! Not even close. You're on the back of the bus that's travelling *behind* the car that your body is driving.

When I started to learn about this, it didn't make sense at all. From what I'd learned growing up and through school, I knew my brain tells my body what to do and my body must listen. My body doesn't have its own brain, does it? Well, not physically, no. But it's very smart. See, when you instruct your body to perform a certain task, like driving, walking the dog around the block or brushing your teeth, your body remembers each step that it takes to do so. Your body is also a very quick learner, so after a few repetitions, you are no longer needed. It does not need the brain to tell it what to do anymore. Once you wake up, your body knows that you have cereal, a coffee and then brush your teeth, so it does just that *for* you. Does this make sense? If not, when was the last time you *consciously* brushed your teeth? Can you actually remember the last time you felt a toothbrush against your canines? Or was your mind too far back, still asleep even, to notice? If you walk your dog around the same block every night, your body remembers the route, each step it takes, each dip in the pavement and each crossing you must take. That's why you'll notice the time the most when you think the most, when you ponder over your life and your worries come back to the surface. It's because your body is doing all the work and your mind is free to be used with no focus on anything else.

Okay, Ben. So, firstly, what the fucking fuck?!
Secondly, are we <u>always</u> on autopilot?
And thirdly, how do we switch it off for good?

Let's say you're walking around the block again and—I'm going to use the scarily accurate phrase here—'minding your own business'. Now, you're on autopilot. All of a sudden, a car pulls out in front of you or a dog appears ahead of you without a collar on or an owner in sight. Then, out comes the mind and out comes *you*. This is what we'll call unfamiliar territory for the body as this is out of routine, and your whole being now needs to make the change from subconscious to conscious, mainly for survival but also partly because it's something your body is facing that it hasn't learned a response to yet. Don't be fooled, though. Yes, you're now out of autopilot and you're behind the steering wheel again, but it's not going to be for long.

Another great example is when you're walking on your own but people are watching. Think walking into a full office or across the playground at school. All of a sudden, you become conscious of the way that you're walking. Autopilot switches itself off and... oh shit... I'm waddling like a pregnant giraffe. Weird, right?

Appreciation is the key to deleting the autopilot button. I've told you that I removed my own ego, but it still appears from time to time, and it's the same with this. Even though I try my absolute best to live *in* each moment and to appreciate every moment, I'm on autopilot a lot too. I've made the same meal every day for weeks now, so I'll admit, I don't cook it consciously!

For you to start being in control and in the driver's seat throughout the day, you need to act like a monk does and really feel each moment. Jay Shetty talks about how he spends a certain amount of time (four seconds, I think) brushing each tooth. He chooses to do this so that the robotic task now becomes a conscious one and one he can really feel. This allows him to *truly* be in the moment, too, and not just pass through life without having actually lived it. Try it yourself! Are there dishes in your sink right now? Go and wash them, but like you've never washed them before. Feel the warm water running off of your fingers, experience the textures when squeezing soap out of the sponge and turn the dishes to the light to make sure all dirt is completely gone and the plates are now cleaner than when you first bought them. Try it the next time you take a shower. Again, really feel the water as it bounces against your head and shoulders, and even have a good old smell of the shampoo that you use.

As a matter of fact, you don't even need to *do* anything. If this is sinking in, then you're already conscious and out of autopilot. Look up from this page and take a few long, slow deep breaths. Look around the room and sit for a minute or two in silence. Let your body do nothing, and if you feel it fighting to do another task, don't give in. You control your body, not the other way around.

Sweet, we're growing. So far, you've learned how and why it's a fantastic idea to question everything in your life, no matter the size of the topic. Questioning our emotions and feelings especially can have a profound effect on our daily lives. You've also questioned how 'time' really works, which shifts your perception and gives you a new lease of life. Good on you. You are now able to recognise when *you* are speaking and also when your ego is speaking, which lets you choose which one to listen to. What's really great is that you're now developing more and more conscious thoughts, which are overtaking your subconscious thoughts, kicking the old 'autopilot you' in the ass! All of this elevates us as humans and helps to take us to new levels, allowing us to be fully present and experience each moment our days bring, ultimately seeking and finding joy in everything! Bravo.

Now, onto the next topic that I'd like to discuss. Again, it's something very familiar to us all, or so we think! The topic is your breath. *Ben, what could you possibly tell me about my own breath that I don't already know?!*

Buckle up.

'TENSION IS WHO YOU THINK YOU SHOULD BE. RELAXATION IS WHO YOU ARE.'

— Chinese proverb

BREATH

Our breath is the only thing that stays with us from the time we enter this body to the time we leave it. Everything else can change, be transfused or transplanted into our bodies, but not the breath, or more specifically, the *way* in which we breathe. Monks have mastered it, yoga utilises it and meditation focuses on it, and now it's your turn.

Here's a quick 'challenge': take the deepest breath that you can right now. Fully inhale and then fully exhale. When was the last time you did that? There are a number of physical health benefits to taking deeper breaths instead of shallow ones, but also mental benefits! Another thing I picked up from Jay Shetty was how controlling our breath allows us to control all our emotions, ultimately controlling our entire life. He explains that when we experience different emotions, our breath changes. Have a quick think and you'll see just how bizarre but true it is. Your breath changes when you're angry, when you're sad, when you're nervous, happy, excited, scared! So, what happens when we learn to take control of our breathing and, like our bodies, kick it out of autopilot? Everything changes.

If you are fully in charge of the way you breathe, then when you face a different emotion, you'll no longer be absorbed by it and you'll become the boss. Imagine continuously taking deep breaths for an hour (not deep enough that you'll pass out, though), and then someone says something to annoy you, or you spend an hour cooking lasagne only to accidentally drop it on the floor. You won't be fazed by it if you continue the same breathing patterns. When you become furious and your breath goes short and sharp, your body can perform a sequence of actions like a domino effect. Your temperature may rise and you may move even quicker and be unable to think clearly, for example. Once you can control it, you become this emotionally invincible being.

The trick to developing an awareness of your own breath is right there in the same sentence. You just need to become *aware* of your breath, in the same way that we've done with using your mind instead of body and using conscious thoughts instead of being mainly subconscious. Of course, there are a number of ways to *learn* how to become aware of your breath and use it properly, like yoga, meditation and tai chi, for example, but the idea behind it all is just noticing your breath. Once you can simply *realise* that you're breathing, your breath changes, doesn't it? Our bodies can be awfully strange. Becoming conscious of your breath really is all it takes to begin to master it, and essentially master your emotions, too.

Tomorrow, wherever you may be, become aware of your breath. Whenever you get a spare conscious moment, as I like to call it, notice how you are breathing, slow it down and visualise the oxygen filling and leaving your lungs. Besides controlling any emotions that may enter from external people and circumstances, you'll also become more centred, grounded and truly in the moment. Give it a try and watch how you change.

'WHY DON'T YOU AND I PLAY A GAME OF 'FUCK OFF'? YOU GO FIRST.'

—Mike Banning, *Olympus Has Fallen*

EMOTIONS

Your emotions are there to guide you, not to control you. Very recently, I became aware that our emotions are actually subconscious responses, 99% of the time. It's pretty obvious when you think about it and how they work, but we never *do* think about it, do we? An emotion is just a 'feeling reaction' or an inner, mental reaction to an event, be it external or internal. Whether someone says or does something to upset you, or you accidentally break something of value to you or you make up a scenario in your head that hasn't even occurred yet: your emotions are just your feelings responding.

What you may not be aware of, however, is that your emotions are big hints that can help you massively once you learn how to read them.

Go on then, Ben. Teach us.

All you need to learn is to separate your emotions from yourself, just like we did with our ego. You can do the same with your thoughts, too, as they also fit the subconscious theme here. Did you know that the average human being has roughly 60,000 thoughts every single day? How many of those can you remember? How many thoughts have you consciously remembered having today? The majority of them are also automatic because they just pop into our heads without us controlling them. This is extremely similar to our emotions, too.

What the emotions do, though, is tell you where you are heading *vibrationally*. You can literally use your emotions as a frequency GPS to understand if you are using the Law of Attraction to your advantage or disadvantage. Let me break it down and relate it to your own life experience.

If you have a negative thought, for example, which is accompanied by a negative emotion, then by the most powerful Universal law, the Law of Attraction, you'll then, unfortunately, continue to attract thoughts of the same negative frequency. Those thoughts will then strengthen that negative emotion and you'll begin the popular term, 'a downward spiral'.

So, let's break it down even further. Let's say that you are feeling unloved and thus you feel emotions associated with loneliness. First, you come to realise that you haven't received a text or phone call from a certain family member in a long time. This thought will attract the same type of thoughts, so then you recall how no one has actually texted or called you in a while. You'll then think of a time when you were unwell and no one reached out to check up on you. This is partly your ego just trying to reaffirm your feeling of being alone because it sees where your thoughts are leading you and it wants to make sure *it* is in control, but mainly because your thoughts magnetically bring more of the same thoughts. Like attracts like. Do you get my point there?

Once you get a grip of those workings of your emotional guidance, you can use them to work in your favour and not against you. How do we do that? By *reading* them. What I mean by that is this:

Let's say that you're trying to manifest money into your life. If you're feeling a joyous emotion around the topic of your financial situation at present, that's *the* sign that an abundance of money is very surely on its way to you. But the other side of the coin is also true: If you're wishing for money to flow into your life but you also feel a negative emotion around your current finances then that's your Inner Being telling you (via your emotions) that you're simply vibrating on the wrong frequency and, therefore, pushing your desired manifestations away from you.

Again, remember that you can *choose* what emotions you want to feel at any given time, so just make sure that when visualising, you're associating happy and joyous emotions with whatever it is that you truly want to attract, keeping in mind that you must also feel that way about your current situation.

'I'VE HAD A LOT OF WORRIES IN MY LIFE, MOST OF WHICH NEVER HAPPENED.'

—Mark Twain

PLACEBO

I wanted to say that this brief section is about a fascinating 'idea' or a concept/theory. If I labelled it as that, however, I'd be lying. It's not an idea, simply a fact.

I assume we've all heard of the 'placebo effect', but for those of you who may be unfamiliar, here's a commonly used example. So, there's a study in which a thousand people are given tablets to take each day to cure their depression. Five hundred of those people are prescribed tablets and told that they're the best tablets you can get. The other five hundred are also told that they're receiving the best tablets in the world, but instead of being given the same tablets as the other half of the experiment, they're just handed sugar tablets. Lo and behold, a few weeks later, once the study had ended, the majority of the participants reported that their depression had lessened and their moods had improved, regardless of what tablet they took.

How can this be possible? How can a person swallow a tablet that's 100% sugar and report that it's started to cure their depression (also other diseases in other studies) just as much as those who took the real tablet? It all comes down to the power of the mind, which we're now going to begin to discuss. I will warn you though: everything you've read so far has been about improving your mindset, outlook and idea of life in general, but now we're about to dive down a rabbit hole. This rabbit hole includes the Law of Attraction, manifestation, affirmations, frequency, vibrations, dimensions and speaking to the Universe itself. Are you ready? Good.

THE TAO THAT CAN BE TOLD IS NOT THE ETERNAL TAO.'

—Lao Tzu

MIND

The reason that a human can swallow sugar and cure their disease is because they *believe* that the tablets will cure the disease. Throughout each of the sections in the rest of this book, the underlying message is the sheer power that the mind possesses. Dr Joe Dispenza wrote a whole book on the topic titled *You Are the Placebo*, and using his ideas, the way I'll now explain how the placebo effect really works will give you the knowledge and freedom to create the exact life it is that you desire. And I mean *really*. This next statement is a bold one and can be very harsh to hear if you know people who've died from certain diseases.

You can eliminate any disease or ailment that resides in your body, instantly, through the power of thought and intention alone.

Your mind and a strong belief are all you need to get rid of what's in your body that isn't working for you. In Dr Dispenza's workshops, some of his students have cured cancer, regained sight and made a number of other diseases disappear. All they did was a few meditations. Don't worry, I *know* it's hard to believe. When I first heard him speak about this, I didn't necessarily lose respect for the guy, but I started doubting what he was all about. I mean, come on, regaining sight and curing cancer just by meditation? Do you have any proof? Yes. Yes, he does. He and a team of scientists really do literally have all the proof. His students have provided scans that show tumours and cancers which, *after* the patient visits one of Dr Dispenza's events, are completely gone in later scans. Define 'a miracle' for me. I'll let you look into Joe, if you haven't already, for more information on those mind-blowing results and how they were achieved (in a week, may I add) but here's my take on the subject, through experience.

Everything in your life is the product of your subconscious mind. We're not going to go *that* deep just yet, but hear me out. A few years ago, at a time when I was training really hard, my aim was just to get stronger and stronger each week. I loved trying to pull heavier weights off the floor during each session, and everyone in my family warned me to be careful in case I damaged my back. Slowly but surely, I started to develop a bad back. It got to the point after a few weeks where I'd wake up in the morning and was almost completely stiff and crippled in pain, even struggling to breathe. I went to see a doctor and was back and forth with a chiropractor, but neither helped. The doctor literally said, 'Don't worry about it, you're young.' Cheers, Doc, problem solved. The chiropractor told me that I'd sprained my back a number of times but my body had carried on until the final sprain, where it couldn't cope. She explained how through the nights, my lower back would tighten, which would even cause my pelvis to lift and twist because of the muscles pulling. I was told it caused one leg to be longer than the other and that I'll be 'fixed' in four sessions, including acupuncture. It didn't help. At the end of the fourth session, where she just assumed that my back was fine, she sent me on my way and recommended that I use a foam roller to help ease the pain. The pain got ever so slightly better, but the morning back pain persisted for years—right up until this year, actually. I'd constantly tell myself and others, and therefore fully believed, that I just *had* to get up and out of bed before 8:00 a.m. because if I stayed in bed for too long, my back would hurt even more so. Before even thinking a conscious or subconscious thought, my brain would immediately find the pain in my lower back as soon as my eyes opened. I'd try to stretch and twist whilst still in bed to ease it but knew deep down that I'd have to get up and go downstairs, where I could fold backwards over the arm of the sofa to ease the pain.

After researching just how powerful the mind is, especially in connection with how self-healing the body actually is, I decided to take things into my own hands. Surely if Dr Dispenza's students can heal diseases that had been deemed incurable, then I could ease a little morning back pain, right?

I no longer have *any* back pain, or any pain at all for that matter. A few months ago, I understood that because we create our own realities, I was *creating*, if you will, my own pain. Just like when we wake up and check our phones to reaffirm to our 'yesterday selves' that the world is still the same and we're the same people we were when we went to sleep, my brain and body simply wanted to confirm that my back still hurt. So, the second I opened my eyes, my entire focus and energy was directed to frantically 'creating' the pain that I had in my back. When I switched up my routine to practising gratitude and visualising before I drifted off and upon waking, I no longer had the time to search for any pain. The pain was almost immediately forgotten about, and in no time it disappeared.

I explained the story about my back to a friend I met up with yesterday, and when I was speaking, and even now as I type, it feels surreal. I eradicated actual, physical pain that lived in my body and arose each morning. Our bodies and minds are seriously astonishing once we harness them. Just take a cut, for example. If you accidentally trip and graze your knee or slip whilst cutting carrots and slice your thumb, your body literally heals it within a few days. If you cut yourself and your skin opens slightly, your body will literally grow it back together and fix the wound itself. That's self-healing, that's crazy.

'PROSPERITY IS YOUR BIRTHRIGHT.'

—Rhonda Byrne

UNIVERSAL

This morning, I sat down with the book *Ask and It Is Given* by Esther and Jerry Hicks. I've always had this idea, since focusing on the origin of my spiritual path, of where I (and you) actually came from. I've always *known* that we aren't human beings that sometimes have spiritual experiences, but rather we are spiritual beings living this experience as human beings. Does that make sense? I mean, at the end of the day, we're all made up of atoms. As a matter of fact, *everything* is made up of atoms. Bob Proctor talks about this perfectly, so feel free to look him up online, mixing science with the Law of Attraction. If you were to look at an atom microscopically, you'd see that it isn't still but is always moving, vibrating even. So, if you look at this book in front of you, no matter how still it may appear to be, underneath what your eyes can see, there is so much movement. Since we're all made up of these atoms, it's scientifically correct to state that our entire body is vibrating, right? That's not mumbo-jumbo talk, that's actual science. I'm telling you this just in case you had a hard time understanding that we are spiritual beings living as humans and not the other way around. The facts about atoms and us being made up of them make you question what we actually are. We're now about to go a little deeper.

Up until a few months ago, I would tell people that my theory about where we 'were' before being on this planet and in this experience was just that: a theory. However, since speaking to the Universe itself (and it speaking back), I can concretely say that my 'theory' is no longer a theory, but the truth.

The book I was reading this morning can be a weird one to get into. The couple who wrote the book, Esther and Jerry, didn't really write it. Well, physically they did, sure—they were the ones who put pen to paper—but the information, teachings and Universal knowledge came from something else. Esther explains how she is able to drop her consciousness down to a level that allows a spirit named Abraham to speak *through* her. Abraham is referred to as 'they' because he's part of a collective consciousness in another dimension, another plane. They speak through Esther from what they call the 'Non-Physical', and the three books of theirs that I've read are truly fascinating and have given me a vast amount of answers to questions I couldn't get answers to elsewhere, and also to questions I didn't even know I had. I'd highly recommend getting yourself a copy of *Ask and It Is Given*, and I'm only one chapter in myself! I'm telling you about this book mainly because when reading today, it seriously backed up the theory that I once had. So, here goes. Have an open mind here and I'll open your eyes.

Before we came into this life, on this planet, as this person and in this experience, we were 'up there'. 'Up there' can be referred to as a number of things: Heaven, Paradise, Source, etc. For me, it's known as the Universe. In this dimension lives pure consciousness itself. This is where we *all* came from, where we'll *all* go back to once our time here is done and where, essentially, we *all* belong. This is what I believe to be the utter truth, but you may personally have a hard time adjusting to it if your theory is different, even more so if you've thought a different way for your entire life. You may be reading this as a religious person and find that what I've just said goes against your faith. Does it, though? Does it really? Firstly, it's great to note that religions and styles/walks of life all preach one thing above all else: **love**. Secondly, what I call the 'Universe' (notice how I capitalise it) can, and is, called many other names, some of which you may even use yourself. Other words for the Universe (the Universe in this sense meaning the dimension that we came from) include Consciousness, Spirit, Source Energy, Higher Power and the most commonly used: God. Depending on your beliefs, you may find it easier to resonate with me more by using 'God' instead of 'Universe'. So, in essence, know that I'm also saying that we came from God, will return to God and we all belong 'up there' with (and as a part of) God. Does that make better sense to you?

This dimension that contains the infinite plane of consciousness and intelligence, which I'll often refer to as the Universe, isn't just that. It's not simply the entire centre of knowledge that we *came* from and *go* to. It's more than that because we have direct access to it right now and not just before and after this life. Each and every one of us has the ability to tap into this abundance of knowledge at any given time. I tapped into it personally and worked with it when I had £200 to my name and was working three jobs. The secrets that I learned allowed me to quit three jobs and spend all day with my daughter, doing whatever I want. I worked with the Universe to manifest £1,000,000 in 45 seconds.

Yes, seconds. I did that by tricking my subconscious into believing that I was *already* a millionaire, which took a month, and then the Universe put an opportunity in front of me that turned £10,000 into £1,000,000 in less than a minute. The Universe/God/Source Energy taught me how and brought it to me. There was me with £200 and a version of me that was a millionaire, and I mentally 'became' the millionaire. In turn, that rapidly attracted this millionaire version of myself to me, which I then actually embodied. The stronger the belief, the stronger the magnet.

The reason we are all able to connect with and contact 'up there' is because part of us (10%, to my understanding) is still up there. The other 90% is here on Earth, so we're still partially connected to our spirit and the collective consciousness up there.

But, this 'dimension'—are there people there? Not exactly, no. There are beings, yes, but not humans like here on Earth. They can communicate with each other and with us and are multidimensional. Think of it as a collective consciousness, or many brains that together make up the all-knowing brain. We're a part of it here in our lives because we originated there, but we were once fully a part of it, we were it itself, if that makes sense. Remember, energy cannot be created or destroyed, only transferred/converted. So why are we here now? We're here on this planet ('planet' is the word 'plane' minus one letter) as this exact person and living this exact life experience because we *chose* to. Before switching dimensions and coming onto this plane, we said to ourselves—and the collective consciousness that we were a part of—that we were going to become a human being on Earth momentarily (in the grand perception of time anyway) and see what things we could learn. We knew that our experience was going to be about having fun as we created whatever life we desired to. We knew that it would be our human *intention* that determined how our lives panned out, and we also knew that the underlying journey would be to seek, keep and spread joy. And here we are. So, now that you're here in this experience, are you seeking joy, creating the life that you desire and learning knowledge through your existence to take back 'up there' with you?

Okay, Ben, your concept of time was great, the ego section really got me, but this is a little out there. How do you know this is the truth and it's not still just a theory that you have?

The Universe and I put this book in your hands, didn't we? The main reason you picked this book up was for self-development, and these kinds of discussions were the last thing you thought you'd read, am I right? This book is in your hands for a reason that you're slowly learning. The Universe wants *you* to learn this. What's so special about you, though? I bet you'll take this knowledge and spread it to as many people as you can. You'll start to find joy and begin to manifest the life that you've always dreamt of, but you won't stop there. You'll create a mini purpose for yourself, making you feel like you *need* to spread the word and help others to find their joy and create their own masterpieces of life. The Universe gave me a lot of money, not only because I asked for it and already believed I had it, but because they just *knew* that I'd tell everyone I could about how I was making a truckload of money without lifting a finger and how they could too, which is exactly what I did.

I also know this to be the truth and no longer just a theory because I experienced it, without knowing what it was. One of the first times I meditated was around eight years ago, and it was a meditation that I'll never forget. My eyes were closed so everything was black, obviously, and I had a candle lit in front of me. Within a few minutes, I was in space. That's the only way I can describe it anyway, the feeling of sitting in the centre of the galaxy. I was sitting on a lily pad, floating in space, and around me were these *incredibly* large figures. I was meditating in my room on campus at university and my friend knocked on the door at that point, so I never found out what would have happened next. The Universe will show you a message in the way that you'll understand it best, so it can be very different from one person to the next. I didn't realise it until recently, but I was connected directly to that plane of consciousness itself during that meditation. I had perfect access to the truth, and although there were zero words exchanged, the presence alone of those beings told me everything that I needed to know. They were there, aware that I only had a few seconds with them, to introduce themselves to me (even though I'd been there before coming into this life and I'd just forgotten) and to give me the feeling that I could connect with them whenever I wanted, that they were waiting for me to do so, and that it wasn't just this plane that existed.

You didn't think I'd go from talking about steroids to that, did you?

This Universal presence is always with me wherever I am and in everything I do. I can be out driving and have a massive smile on my face as though I've just won billions on the lottery, for no other reason other than I *know* the truth. I sincerely feel as though I've unlocked the secrets of how the world really works, like entering cheat codes into a video game. Need more money? Believe you have it and it'll come. Need to get your health in check? Believe you're as fit as a fiddle and it'll come. Waiting for that perfect partner? Believe you've just met your perfect match and they'll appear before you can finish this book. Yesterday whilst with my friend, after speaking about the Law of Attraction and how you can and *do* continuously create your own reality, I then spoke about how other people in our hometown made a lot of money just by copying what I did and investing in the stocks that I did. If I haven't mentioned it yet, I made the majority of my money in the stock market, and I know *nothing* about the stock market. I told my friend about one guy who'd messaged me asking for investing advice (I never had any advice, but whenever I told the hundreds of people messaging me that they could manifest money instead, they didn't want to know) and this guy had been in school with us and was rather horrible to me in particular. As I said his name and our brains took us back momentarily to the emotions that we'd felt in school, the same guy drove around the corner and appeared in front of us. This is due to nothing other than the fact that you can literally put anything you want right in front of you. You can create an image in your mind and it'll physically manifest almost quite literally right before your eyes. *That's* the power of the mind and that's the power of the Universe.

I bet, if you think about it, something similar has happened to you, too. Before I give you an example for you to relate to, just know that that guy appeared in front of me instantly because I've learned to work directly with this Universal power/being and have full belief in its workings. You may not have that belief just yet, but you *are* manifesting and creating your own reality subconsciously. The only difference between me and you up until this point in your journey is I'm now creating *consciously*. I can't wait for you to do the same.

So, the example. Have you ever been driving down the road and you'll see a car that you're about to pass and you recognise it as, let's say, an old friend's car? The car gets closer and passes and you realise that it's not actually them. However, a few hours later, or even on the same road, you *do* see them. This has happened to you, hasn't it? Coincidence, right? If you haven't already, you'll soon come to learn that there are no coincidences. Have you ever sat and thought about how you haven't seen a certain someone in a long time, only to see them a day or two later? That's because you *literally* put that person in front of you. You held an image of them in your mind that was based on seeing that person, and the Universe made it so.

As I'm sure you already know, I love Marvel. What I will say, however, is *this* is the best superpower to have. Not super-strength, not flight, and definitely not laser eyes. Harnessing the mind and the power of the Universe? You'd beat all the heroes. Even Spidey. If this whole thing *is* true and you really *can* create your own reality just by believing that all of your desires have already manifested, the question now is *how*.

Let me teach you.

‘I’M NOT WHAT I THINK I AM, I’M NOT WHAT YOU THINK I AM, I AM WHAT I THINK YOU THINK I AM.’

—Charles Cooley

AFFIRMATIONS

I am...

What are affirmations? You can Google the literal meaning, which is rather boring, but for me, and in regard to manifesting, here's how I describe it: An affirmation is a statement that you write down and read over and over again until you believe it's true. It's all about attracting something into your life that you desire, by acting and believing as though you already have it. Sounds easy, right? Always write the desire down in present tense as though it is already a fact and the thing has already manifested itself in your life, and then read it over to *affirm* it. In this section, I'll teach you how to use affirmations to your advantage and how to trick your brain into believing that you already drive that Lamborghini you want.

When I first picked up a few books and began to read about the Law of Attraction, they all taught how important it was to put pen to paper when creating your affirmations. It was summer at the time, and when I was reading, I'd be out in the garden catching some rays (and asking Jess to take photos of me topless to feed my ego). Due to the fact that I was relaxed and outdoors when reading, there was no way that I'd actually listen to the book and get up to go back into the house, find a pen, find a notepad and then return to the garden just to write something down, only to read it. The way I saw it was if they wanted me to write it down to just read it out, surely, I could just read it in my head without actually getting up and writing it down? My list of affirmations (that were in my head and not on paper) manifested very quickly, but in slightly different ways than I had asked for and believed in. Once I wrote this list down on paper, things changed drastically. I tell everyone that I know that they should use affirmations to their advantage, and even doing it for a day or two will bring astonishing results into your life. I tell them all the easiest and most effective way to use them, which is this:

I want you to write down a list of ten things. Five of those things must already be true in your life and five of those things should be things that you desire, but you should write them as though they were already also true. For example:

I am Ben Cole-Edwards.

I am successful.

I am wealthy.

I am happy.

I have the perfect relationship with Jess.

I have two healthy dogs, Romeo and Cooper.

I take on one client every day.

I own a Range Rover Sport.

I am healthy.

I have made it.

This is near enough word-for-word how my first list went. It wasn't perfect, but nevertheless, it worked. You don't need to create a new list every day either—that's a common question I get. Once you've set your mind on your list of desires, if they don't change, keep going over the same list. If you think of something else you'd like to add, add it. Sometimes, when trying to manifest something really big, I *do* like to write the same goal down as an affirmation over and over each day. Notice how I start with my name, too. Doing this sets the list off in the best way possible because you're stating something that is undoubtedly true and your brain knows that it's impossible for that to be a lie. When you immediately read out the next affirmation, your brain will continue to read it as if it is true, even if it's a big desire of yours that you haven't yet accomplished.

Practise this technique whenever you get a spare conscious moment. Personally, I find that you don't need to read it off of the paper each time and can go over it in your head once it's down on paper. I've mentioned too how it's important to write the affirmation in present tense. A lot of people that come to me and say they've tried it out but have had no joy in doing so have also been writing 'I'm going to make £1,000,000' instead of 'I *have* £1,000,000'. If you write as though it's something that's coming, it will always be just out of reach. Have you kept telling yourself that you are going to find the perfect partner? *Going to?* You'll be forever waiting.

Practising your affirmations is an exercise that you can perform out loud, but doing it in your head means that you can do it literally anywhere. I'd be walking down the aisle at work, and in my head, I'd be saying, *'I'm Ben Cole-Edwards. I'm a fucking millionaire.'* I've added swearing in there for a good reason, too. You need to write down and say your affirmations like you would naturally say them. You might find a good affirmation that you've heard from a guru, but it doesn't feel like something you'd normally say. That's absolutely fine, just change it. I like to say, 'I have an abundance of money. Money flows into my life daily and in increasing amounts.' I got the idea of that particular one from hearing Bob Proctor say some of his affirmations that didn't quite resonate with me, so I reworded them. The Universe won't judge you for swearing; it already knows who you are because you *are* it. If you feel a more joyous emotion by saying something like, 'My name is Anne and I'm filthy fucking rich, yeah babyyyy!!' then so be it, no harm done. Emotion is the key word there, too. It's fantastic to practise your affirmations, and doing so will work absolute wonders, but the emotions that you feel when saying them play a much bigger role. So, let's talk about how to manifest them correctly.

'IF IT ENTERTAINS YOU NOW BUT WILL BORE YOU SOMEDAY, IT'S A DISTRACTION. KEEP LOOKING.'

—Naval Ravikant

MANIFESTATION

The underlying emotion beneath whatever it is you say is what the Universe hears and feels. You can sit in a field in deep meditation, even with a smile on your face, and scream to the Universe, 'I'm rich! I'm rich! I'm rich!' but how you really *feel* underneath that sentence determines what your magnet attracts. You can yell from the rooftops that you have an unlimited supply of money as much as you like, but if you feel broke on the inside and feel as though it's *not* having money that's the issue, then nothing will change.

The Universe speaks amongst itself, collectively, and also speaks to you and me. It's speaking to you through this book and is available to communicate with whenever you desire. The thing is though, it doesn't speak via language. It simply conveys a message in a way that you'll understand. The Universe *can* speak to you through actual words, but it'll appear in something random. There was a time when I was a delivery driver and one day it was as though the radio was speaking to me. It honestly felt like someone was pulling a prank on me, because nearly every lyric responded to me, my thoughts and my emotions. Something inside me told me that the messages and words I was receiving weren't coincidental, and most certainly weren't from this plane. I was approaching a roundabout as I said aloud, 'If anyone's doing this to me, give me a sign!' As I came to a stop on the roundabout, there was a massive billboard in front of me, which in big letters read, 'ARE YOU READING THE SIGNS?' I didn't know what to do from there and left it alone in my mind for years. Who could I tell that to?! The Universe will also give you synchronicities to let you know that your manifestations are on their way. Like when you add to your list of affirmations 'I own a Ferrari' and then out of nowhere you begin to see them everywhere. Or when you keep saying 'I'm a millionaire' and you switch on the TV and the program playing is *Who Wants to Be a Millionaire?*

I'm explaining the way in which the Universe communicates with us all so that we can now learn how to communicate with *it*! So, if this collective being, this entity that basically grants us all of our wishes, *doesn't* speak English, how are we supposed to ask it for something? Two words:

Underlying emotion.

Your words: *I have an abundance of money.*

Your underlying emotion: *I need more money.*

Which one there do you think the Universe hears? I say 'hears', but the closest word would be 'feels'. In this example, all the Universe hears is 'I need more money', or better yet, the feeling of lacking money. I'm going to label 'lack' as an emotion here, and it's an emotion that you should stay very far away from. To better understand how manifesting works best and how dangerous lack is, imagine that the way you attract your goals is through a big emotion magnet. This is really called frequency, but emotion magnet fits perfectly here. Quick examples: if you're feeling joy, you attract joy, and if you're feeling like money is flowing into your life, money will continue to flow into your life. Can you see where I'm going here? Verbally declaring your financial abundance is great, but if you feel lack underneath those words, that is what you'll *really* attract. Feeling like you have a lack of money can and will *only* bring you more 'lack of money', it's that simple. I'd even encourage you to put this book down now and practise this section on its own for a few days before coming back to it. The Law of Attraction has been working for you throughout your entire life and is completely unbiased: it gives *you* what *you* give it. Knowing this fact means that you can now choose to *consciously* create, and not just subconsciously like you've been doing up until now.

To speed up the manifestation of your affirmations, feel the emotion that you'd feel when you *do* accomplish it. If one of your affirmations is 'I own a villa with a pool in Barcelona', but you actually only have £3.50 to your name and still live with your parents, that's absolutely fine. In fact, that's amazing! The key here, though, is to truly *feel* the way that you'd feel when picking up the keys to your villa, paying in cash and seeing your own pool for the first time. That's when you'll be able to begin to be grateful for things that you haven't even got! That may not even sound possible from your current perspective, but now, you're about to learn how you can mentally 'live' and 'remember' your future.

‘FLOW SPELLED BACKWARDS IS WOLF.’
—Alex Huberman

FUTURISTIC

If you can get behind the literal fact that energy can't be created nor destroyed, and we're all made of that same energy, then hear this: everything that has ever happened, and everything that is going to happen, is all happening right now, alongside this moment. Parallel, if you will. We've briefly touched upon the 'past' and 'future' in the first section on time, but let's explore the concept a little further. When you think of a past traumatic event, you mentally return to that point in time or, perhaps more fittingly, *emotionally revisit* that moment. You can vividly see the event happening in your mind and can feel all the emotions that you felt at that time. That makes it real, does it not? That's how your brain knows that it actually happened because you can visually and emotionally recall it.

So, here's a question: what if you did the same thing about the future? What if you 'recalled', which in this sense is to imagine or recreate, a scenario in the future? Do this with an affirmation that you have. Imagine that house being yours, imagine picking up that supercar, see it happening and, most importantly, feel the emotions that you're going to feel when it *does* actually manifest. Your brain is unable to tell the difference between reality and imagination. If you continue to imagine that you are already that wealthy and healthy 'future you', and really feel like it's true, then your brain doesn't know that it's not yet the truth. Once you've convinced yourself and your brain that what you want to come true has actually already come true, the Universe makes it so.

For me, my future genuinely does seem just as real as my past. Actually, the majority of my past seems like a blur, as it was mainly on autopilot. My future, however, is crystal clear. Here's a little personal insight: I'm currently manifesting a supercar that I want, but there's a list of things I want first, so even though I could buy it now, I won't. Let me explain. Jess and I are trying for another baby, and our next phase is vaguely this: baby, travel for a few years with the children and dogs, return, buy a house, and *then* buy my Lamborghini. I wouldn't want one where we currently live, and we're not set on an area where we want to live just yet—not set enough to buy a home there, anyway. I'd love a villa in Valencia, while Jess wants to move less than a mile away, which is why we'll travel first so we can decide. Aaaanyway, I'm still trying to manifest the Lamborghini, not just because I'll own the supercar, but because owning it means that I'd have accomplished everything else first! I love paddleboarding and go most mornings depending on the weather. I say I love it—I actually just love sitting on the water because it brings me joy (and peace), and a paddleboard allows me to do just that. The majority of the time, when walking back to the car from the sea, I <u>fully</u> believe that I'm going to see my supercar instead of my actual car. Like, I really do expect to pull out the Lamborghini key and get in it. I've actually driven the Lamborghini that I want, but I 'remember' driving it in the future more than when I actually drove it in the past. This is the case because I'm almost fully living in my future, I'm *that* certain about it.

The closer that 'future you' feels to 'current you', the faster your dreams will manifest. The best technique you'll learn in this book, which I used and will continue to use to attract my future and be *in* my future, is visualisation.

'IT GETS BETTER WHEN YOU DO.'

—Ben Cole-Edwards

VISUALISATION

Don't be confused here—visualising is just a posh word for imagining that us Law-of-Attraction preachers use to make us sound more enlightened. My imagination has always been insane, if I do say so myself. My family will tell you the same, too. I was always writing stories (mainly about me and my mates getting superpowers) and I could create stories like it was nothing. Due to this, I found visualisation very easy from the moment I tried it. However, after coaching others how to use visualisation to materialise their manifestations, I can give you the beginner's guide. Like the majority of things I've explained in this book, though, you've already been visualising your reality, whether it's been to your advantage or not. Like when you go for a job interview and don't get it, that's only because you didn't *see* yourself in that position. Without even knowing about the Law of Attraction and true power of visualisation, whenever I'd apply for a job, I'd always unintentionally visualise myself working at that place, earning the wage that went with it and imagining the things that I'd buy with it. I've had 11 jobs from the ages of 17–25, and there wasn't a single job that I was rejected from.

Visualisation was the one technique, above all else, that brought my desires to me the fastest. The second half of *Retired At 25* contains *all* of the techniques that I use to manifest my dreams, and in it, I explain to the reader that they should try each one and then choose the ones that felt best to them. Visualisation is the technique that stuck with me and had the quickest and biggest results. I began by visualising that I was going to receive £1000, when I only had £200 to my name. I created the feeling within myself that I had already received the money, and held the feeling of being rich within my body. I even imagined what I'd spend the money on when the Universe gave it to me. The thing that worked best and felt the strongest was when I closed my eyes and visualised myself opening up the online banking app on my phone and seeing £1200 instead of £200. Three days later, I had an email from the government stating that as my personal training business was taking less money due to COVID, I was entitled to a grant. Guess how much the grant was? £1046. I wonder why the Universe tipped me £46! I'll admit that I thought of it as a coincidence, but then I manifested a car and a £950,000 house. Here's where I visualised wrong though. I wanted this silver Audi A4 that I'd seen for sale online and was out of my budget. I'd imagine it outside my house, just sitting there as though I was looking at it through the bedroom window. The same week, I opened my front door to leave the house and there was this silver Audi A4 parked right outside. What had happened there? An actual coincidence? But I was being taught through all these books that there are no coincidences. My neighbour asked me who the car belonged to, and I smiled and said I had no idea. I went back to the same book that I'd been reading and on the next page was the answer. This has always been the same since I started to learn about this Universal power: whenever I needed an answer or guidance, I'd pick up the book that I was reading and almost immediately find the answer I was looking for. Another way that the Universe communicates with me. This time, after the car appeared, the book explained that when you're visualising, you need to be really specific, and even include your senses. The author literally said that you can't just imagine a car outside your house, but you *in* the car, with the feeling that it *is* yours. The book, which if I recall correctly was *Good Vibes, Good Life* by Vex King, explained that whilst visualising, you should also hear the engine of the car, feel the leather on the steering wheel and always have the image in first person, because that's how you'd see it anyway.

I tried again, but to manifest something bigger. I'd manifested a few smaller things after seeing the Audi outside, but I wanted to see if I could really take it to the next level. There was this house that I'd seen that was up for sale for £950,000. I had less than £2000. The three-story house had a view of the sea and was around a 30-minute drive from my current house, and for some bizarre reason, I tried to manifest it. Every morning, I'd get up and go straight downstairs to sit at the dining table with a cup of tea. I'd listen to "What a Wonderful World" by Louis Armstrong and visualise the house. One of the photos of this house that was on the 'for sale' advert was a photo of its balcony, overlooking the ocean. So, I'd be sitting at my table drinking tea and listening to that song, but I'd have my eyes closed. In my mind, I'd be sitting on the balcony of the £950,000 house, looking out at the sea whilst drinking a cup of tea and listening to the same song. I wasn't even sure why I was doing it as the house was so expensive to me at the time, but I think I wanted to visualise one big thing for however long it took. After two weeks of doing this for literally four or five minutes (the length of the song) each morning, I headed out to attend to two clients who had booked me in for Swedish massages. At the end, one of the clients thanked me and told me she wanted to book me in for every other week. This would be my first regular client, so I was over the moon. She then asked if I'd be willing to go to her new house if she paid me extra. I asked where and she told me. It was the same place that the £950,000 house was. I explained that I had been looking at one for sale in that area, dreaming, and told her the price. She said, 'Yeah, that's the one.' It was the exact house. I'd been visualising myself on the balcony of that house for two weeks and just like that, I'd be in it! As you can tell though, I made the same mistake as the Audi: it wasn't *mine* in my visualisation. This was the moment that I erased the word 'coincidence' from my vocabulary (other than when saying there aren't any). This was a clear sign from the Universe that I could literally have whatever I wanted, I just had to visualise it right. A few months later, I quit three jobs because I had the financial freedom to do so.

'THE THREE BIG ONES IN LIFE ARE WEALTH, HEALTH AND HAPPINESS. WE PURSUE THEM IN THAT ORDER, BUT THEIR IMPORTANCE IS REVERSE.'

—Naval Ravikant

ONE

If, as I hope, you're now getting behind that idea that we have originated from the same system and are currently branches of the same tree, you'll soon come to realise that we're all one. Every single one of us here on Earth drinks from the same river of consciousness, and therefore, we are all different versions of the same Source and merely living different experiences. Knowing this, would you now want to treat anyone/ *everyone* differently? There's a theory, and it is only theory (but does make a lot of sense), that you live as every single person on this plane, one by one. Once you have lived as each of the billions of humans, you become God. This is not too far from what I'm saying anyway, but it definitely makes you think, doesn't it?

So, if everyone is me and I am everyone, then how should we go about treating everyone? We've all heard the quote 'treat others as you wish to be treated' and even the quote spanning all the way back to 'Love thy neighbour'. The best way I learned to love everyone, and I can't remember where I read it, is to act as though every person you meet is your child or mother. I laughed when it was first introduced to me. So, you're telling me that you want me to act like I'm the father to the old women that I work with? Get out of here! What helps with this is combining it with the concept of time. If you struggle to see some random stranger as your offspring, then ignore the idea of age. Essentially, forget about how many times someone has orbited the sun.

I used to hate crowds. I remember this one time I was away with Jess and her family, around four years ago, and we were in an indoor space, about to go into another room to see the entertainment of the night. There were people everywhere. I always knew that I didn't like being in a crowd, but this was the first time I'd ever had a panic attack. The vast amount of people in one space affected my breathing and sense of safety. How is that even possible?! Oh yeah, because I wasn't in control. Even when I worked in the supermarket, crowds just frustrated me. At a certain time most days, just after the local school had closed for the day, there'd be a rush of customers. I no longer panicked in crowds, but I just got angry for no reason. Or was it the steroids… Now, however, I love (maybe too strong a word) crowds. Again, when you change the way you look at things, the things you look at change. I altered my perspective and began to see each individual as a part of this family. I say 'this' family instead of 'my' family because they don't feel like brothers and sisters as such, but more like cogs in the same machine, if you will. Some of those cogs are bigger and therefore play a more important role in the machine and some cogs are small and don't really do much, but each one is needed to keep the machine running.

Once you begin to see everyone as an extension of yourself, you're able to see why they do certain things. I can't even see a person as a person anymore, because I automatically look deep into the way they do things and analyse why they've done what they've done in their lives. I can be in a shop and ask a member of staff how their day is going and they'll respond with, 'Same shit, different day.' I normally just laugh it off, but on the inside, I want to respond by saying, 'Actually, the day is exactly how you make it. You've created a "shit" day subconsciously before this day even arrived, but you have the choice to actively seek out the joy and positive aspects of this "shit" day. All you have to do to respond with "I'm having a great day" is believe that the day you wake up to will be utterly fantastic.' But I don't want to sound like I've *completely* lost the plot now, do I? All you have to do to change a person's day, and potentially their life, for the better is to pass on a smile, crack a joke or pay a compliment. Changing someone's mood can do *so* much.

If we began to see the people in our surroundings as part of our 'family' and realise that we've all relatively recently come from the plane of pure consciousness, *and* we begin to treat and speak to everyone in a different manner, we spread positivity to the people around us.

‘THAT WHICH WE ARE SEEKING IS SEEKING US.’

—Dr Joe Dispenza

NEGATIVITY

I switch between two views on negativity, depending on the person and circumstance, but the two views work well together. In short, one view is 'If someone's negative towards me, then they have their own reasons deep down as to *why* they aren't spreading positivity,' and the other is 'Fuck you.' Let's explore both, shall we?

Once you start questioning the reasons for things wherever and whenever you can, especially in your own life and emotions, you'll come to understand that everyone has their own reasoning behind negative words. What I mean by this is that if *you've* ever been negative or said something nasty to someone else and then looked back to question *why* you said those things, you may find a deep-rooted reason. These reasons, though, are almost all of the time backed by the ego.

When I first deposited money into my trading account and told my mother, she explained that it was 'gambling' and that I didn't know what I was doing. In all fairness, I *didn't* know what I was doing, but the Universe did. My mother saying those words wasn't actually her speaking, but the prejudice of her ego. She said, 'That's gambling and you don't know what you're doing,' but she actually meant '*I* don't know how to invest and potentially make a lot of money without doing any work, so *you* shouldn't know how to do that either and it would be selfish of you to make money without me knowing how to do the same and me being the one who does it first.' My mother's words were just a defence mechanism for her ego, and she didn't even know it.

When I worked one factory job, there was this guy there who always hit the gym to train arms, and nothing else. Each to their own and all, but his ego always wanted him to forget that he had skinny legs, so he'd call out other people for flaws in their bodies. I'd post photos of me topless at the gym (which was also ego-driven) and he'd comment saying 'Haha, why don't you post photos of your legs.' He *said* that, yes, but what he really conveyed was his own insecurities. He was also a personal trainer but had zero clients, so when I was posting progress photos of my own clients, and then photos of myself, his ego forced him to speak up and be negative towards me in the hope that it'd block out what he saw as his own flaws.

The sad thing is the majority of people don't break out of this negative state because they aren't aware that they are able to do so or are even aware that they're doing it because it's an autopilot defence mechanism of the ego. All it takes is to question it. There are a number of reasons why people are negative towards you, so here they are, broken down:

YOU ATTRACTED A NEGATIVE VIBRATION

Is there someone that you work with, or even a bunch of people, that aren't very nice to you? Maybe they criticise the way you act, the way you look or even the way in which you work. If you experience that negative energy a handful of times, and unfortunately feel as though you are unable to remove yourself from that situation each day, then your brain will constantly seek it out each time you get to work. You will have lowered your own vibration and are now on that lower frequency of negativity. You are now 50/50 subconsciously and consciously creating each shift that you work. You receive verbal abuse every day, and so you begin to expect it and, therefore, create it. A family member will ask how your job is going and you'll mentally reinforce it by saying 'The people there aren't very nice to me,' or you'll turn into the 'Same shit, different day' colleague.

If this is you, then there is only one way for it to stop: create it so. Create the day, create your upcoming shift in your head and remove those negative thoughts that those people usually verbalise in your direction. Stop expecting it and start giving gratitude for a fantastic job where you can be your true self freely and without worry of judgement.

YOUR OWN FEELINGS OF NEGATIVITY GIVEN BACK TO YOU

Another reason people may be negative towards you, which is the hardest to identify for many people, is that *you're* a negative person and say horrible things to others. It's hard to identify because nasty people never feel nasty. I know because I was one of them. Up until the age of around 14-15, I feel as though I never really had a conscience and I'd be nasty to people for no reason. A lot of it was because I was bullied in school myself, so maybe I thought that was the way it had to be or maybe I wanted revenge. A best friend of mine, from the age of around ten to this present day, is someone that I was nasty to when I was younger. Looking back, I think I perceived certain things I did as pranks, but it was definitely me just not being a nice person. One time, whilst waiting for the school doors to open, I sprinted towards him from behind and tackled him to the floor, for absolutely no reason. I think I just wanted to be considered funny to others and impress girls, but I had no idea why it would have achieved anything even remotely similar to that result. I can see now just how cruel that was, but I had no idea then, which is why it's hard for people to identify that they keep facing negative circumstances because *they* are negative too.

A person who is constantly negative has lowered their vibration. This means that everything they attract into their own lives will be on the same frequency of negativity and nastiness. If this is you—and congratulations for owning up to it—the only way to get out of this is to raise your own vibration (which I'll talk about very soon) and start spreading positive words and having thoughts of positivity and joy, ultimately attracting the same back to yourself.

YOUR EGO CONFIRMING YOUR INSECURITIES

I hate to keep talking about how skinny my legs were, but it's very relevant here. I used to hate wearing shorts. Even when I was taking steroids and had 'decent'-sized legs, I would only wear a particular length of shorts because otherwise, someone would always comment on how thin they were. Can you guess why different people kept negatively commenting on my legs each time I wore shorts? Yes, because I kept attracting their negative words. How did I 'make' them say those hurtful words? There are two reasons. Number one, as the subtitle suggests, it was *me* who really felt the negative thoughts about my own body, so my ego wanted to make sure I knew that I was right. I would feel like I was literally *waiting* for at least one person to mention it every time. The second reason is that like attracts like, so whatever you think about, you bring about. The moment I'd step out in public with a pair of shorts on, there was <u>nothing</u> on my mind besides how insecure I was about my legs.

Imagine how I felt when I realised that I was putting all of my mental energy into that one predominant thought and how phenomenal it would be if I simply did that with a positive thought or affirmation! The Universe was simply reading my main thought, which in this case was 'Everyone's looking at, and are going to comment on, my legs,' and made it so.

So, if we can now see that we can vibrate on a range of different frequencies, how do we control or navigate them? How can we 'vibrate higher' and change our reality by doing so? Luckily for you, you've picked up the right book.

‘YOUR PAST DOES NOT EQUAL YOUR FUTURE.’
- Tony Robbins

FREQUENCY

Every guru, author and coach uses the same example here, so it would be rude of me not to do the same. The easiest and most efficient way of teaching this is to relate it to something simple. A radio. Back in the day, there was just 'the' radio, but now there are radios on our phones and even in our cars, and we all know how they work, right? When using a radio, if you want to receive different information to what you're currently getting, you just turn the dial and tune in to another frequency. And as we all know, when you're tuned in to one frequency, you don't receive any information from any other frequency. So, if there is a radio station that plays rock music on 108 and you were in the mood for rock music, you'd tune to 108. If there was a station that played something a little more classical on 102.3, and that was something that tickled your fancy, you'd simply tune your radio to 102.3. Now you can agree with me here when I say that you won't hear any rock music whilst you're tuned into 102.3, right? It works the same way with our own inner frequency, and it's also just as simple. The highest frequency is pure joy, and the lowest is pure hatred for life itself. This may sound a little easy here, but to raise your frequency, you just need to be more consistently in a state of joy so the Universe can bring you more and more of that joy.

With the negativity scenario, even if that money/ health/happiness is flowing into your life, whilst you're still on that low frequency, you can only attract more negativity and lack. This is what I was explaining earlier with underlying emotions. Speaking wondrous things and affirming your dream life is all well and good, but if you feel broke underneath then you're on the frequency of lack, and the Universe can only give you more 'lack of' whatever it is. It/They match your frequency. You tune into the Universe's lowest level frequency and unfortunately begin to receive all that it has to offer.

Let's say you're at a family gathering and a family member says something that annoys or upsets you. What happens then? Your frequency lowers—if you allow it to, that is. It can be a dangerous slide from there if you're not careful. One negative thought brings on another and then another and before you know it, you've slipped into a slight depression. You'll really feel the harsh words that you've received and then you'll begin to think of all of the negative things that that person has said to you before. Then you'll think of other family members and recall any nasty comments they have made. Whenever someone makes a horrible remark, you'll survey the room to see who smiles or laughs in agreement. Do you see how this works?

Remember that your thoughts usually enter your mind without you consciously thinking them. The way to overcome or even prevent this 'bad mood' is to stop yourself tuning into the wrong frequency; you can begin to *choose* to feel good emotions, and you'll slowly but surely climb back up the ladder (not even slowly, if you do it right). That's the *how* of this whole thing, to *choose* what it is that you want to feel. If you know that you need to be vibrating on the highest and most enlightened frequency there is to achieve your dreams, then *do* something about it. And do something about it right now. I often find that I'll pick up a book and after a paragraph or two, I'll decide that putting the book down and visualising my future will raise my frequency higher, so I come back to the book at another time. I'm saying this because this book isn't going anywhere. I'm flattered if you truly are receiving knowledge that you resonate with here in this book and are eager to read on, but don't forget to get out there and practice the techniques, too! It brings me so much joy to see more and more young people practising this and beginning to talk about sensing peoples' energies and 'reading the room'. Do you know that the word 'vibe', which is getting more and more mainstream, is literally short for the word 'vibration'? We're getting close!

Another thing that slows the manifestation train is worrying. I read a great quote today in the book *Ask and It Is Given* by Esther and Jerry Hicks:

'Worrying is using your imagination to create something you don't want.'

How wonderful and so perfectly put is that? Worrying *literally* does nothing for you and there isn't a single benefit in doing so. I mean, really take a second to think about it here. When you are worrying about something, it's something that has yet to (and may not even) actually happen. Also, as we now know, this is a form of visualisation. Like the quote says, you're actually creating, designing and manifesting a future scenario that you do not want. No matter what you put your focus and intention on, if you're majorly worrying about something then you'll be on the frequency of worry and thus attract whatever it is you're worrying about.

'THE BEST WAY TO FIND YOURSELF IS TO LOSE YOURSELF IN THE SERVICE OF OTHERS.'

—Mahatma Gandhi

HOW

Rhonda Byrne's book *The Secret* teaches that 'prosperity is your birthright'. If this is truly the case for each and every one of us and not just a select few, *how* do we achieve it? That's the wrong question. After I manifested a **lot** of money, I continued to try and manifest more. What I was focusing on and where I held my energy, however, was in the stock market, not the end result, which is the wrong way to manifest. In my head, I'd be visualising a certain value of money, and to achieve that I felt as though a certain stock I'd invested in would have to hit a share price of X amount, simply because I couldn't see any other way that a larger sum of money would appear. This then meant that whenever the share price of said stock would drop, my mood and ultimately, my frequency, would lower drastically, almost exactly in direct correlation to the share price. I'd think that my manifestations weren't coming because I believed that they just *had* to come from that one thing! When I then manifested twenty times the money that I had, it wasn't in my stocks. In fact, when I began making a lot more money via another way, where I made the million in under a minute, I couldn't have cared less about the stock market! Funny that.

My point here is to forget about the 'how'. The Universe takes care of the how. When I manifested the £1046 at the start of my conscious Law of Attraction journey, I had at first doubted that the money would come because I couldn't think of *how* it could come. I first thought it'd be a result of me taking on more online clients, then I thought maybe I would just be doing a lot of overtime in the supermarket, and out of nowhere came an email about being entitled to a grant! Forget about *how* it's going to happen and start focusing on the *end result.* Use visualisation to *see* yourself having already manifested all of your affirmations, and you won't need to worry about the how. The key is belief. Know that what you desire is, and always has been, on its way to you, and now you're just speeding the whole thing up.

Last November, after making £20,000–£30,000 so far in the year, I added to my list of affirmations, 'I make £60,000 this year.' I doubted it, yet again, but a few weeks later, the Universe handed me £250,000 instead. This happened because the Universe put an opportunity in front of me. I had £8700 in one stock, which was 99% of my net worth, and everything lined up to show me another stock. There was a 'top winners' section on my trading platform that I'd never even seen before, so I checked it out. At the top was this penny stock trading at 14c a share and was already up 91% that day, which absolutely baffled me. Seeing a penny stock with such a high daily gain would turn any experienced investor away, but I, not knowing a single thing about the stock market, threw all of my £8700 in, turning it into £250,000 in five weeks! That was the last thing that I'd thought was going to happen when I wrote it down to affirm it, but the Universe thought of it, and the Universe aligned it to make it so. By eliminating any theories or doubts in regard to *how* it's all going to manifest, and by simply focusing on the final picture, you allow your desires to arrive faster.

'MY RELIGION IS VERY SIMPLE. MY RELIGION IS KINDNESS.'

—Dalai Lama

WISDOM

Now that you've picked up a number of vital techniques and insights into the true workings of your own being, I'm sure you have a growing list of questions for me, and for yourself. What may be strange to understand at first, and you may already know where I'm going here, is that you already have all of the answers.

You see, you *are* the answer. You are It. You are Everything. That place that you materialised from, the place that you will also return to, still flows through you right this second. You are consciousness *itself* and thus know all that there is to know. Now, it's not easy to 'remember' something that you don't know you already know, but the answers will come flowing into your very being once you embrace your truth.

Take a moment to repeat these following affirmations:

I am the Universe.

The Universe flows through me.

The creative power of my mind is the Universal Law of Attraction flowing through me.

I *am* the Universe.

I am.

Do those affirmations feel good to say? They should. You can forget all of my teachings if you can simply learn the almighty fact that you *are* everything and everything is a reflection of you.

That's fantastic, Ben, I really feel empowered and all, but how do I really ***find*** *the answers? Does the universe have Google?*

You'll be surprised to know that the answer is almost a yes—something along those lines anyway. Do you have questions burning at the back of your mind that you can't quite figure out the answers to? Is it something about your true calling or your purpose here on Earth? Do you know why you've never found the answers to those certain questions? You've never asked! Think about it for a second! Have you ever wondered what your Inner Being's goals are whilst here on this plane? Have you pondered your entire existence and realised that you must have been sent here to do something? Then why haven't you asked those questions?! Of course, the answer here is very simple. You've never known *who* to ask, have you? Okay, so listen to this. You need to ask yourself, but *through* the Universe. That's how you 'remember' what you've simply forgotten.

Ben, I need answers, tell me howwwww!!!

Ask for a sign.

Ask for a what?!

I've already mentioned this, but I want to talk about the first sign that I received from the Universe after I asked it (without even knowing who I was asking) for one.

I get a lot of signs, and I mean a lot, through music. Whenever I've felt stuck or am undecided regarding certain situations in my life, music has always spoken to me. And I don't just mean that I've been sad and there's a sad song on the radio. When I was working in the supermarket and faced mental predicaments, the radio would seem to grow louder (because I hadn't consciously been aware of it before) and the first lyrics that I'd hear would give me the answers that I needed. I can recall a time when I was stressed out, and I can't even remember what about now, and the lyrics that 'appeared' were: 'Don't you worry 'bout a thiiiing.' It really does put a smile on your face once you know that you have the Universe's direct phone number.

Even before this, and before my whole journey began, the Universe delivered my first *literal* sign. I was working as a courier and was facing a big emotional dilemma. Throughout one day, the radio was speaking to me directly. It got to the point where, as I told you earlier, I genuinely thought that I was being pranked because the lyrics in the songs that were playing made too much sense for it to all be a coincidence. The sign that the Universe gave me was so revolutionary that I can't remember the songs that were playing or even the challenge that I was facing at the time. For example, though, imagine delivering a parcel to a house with the customer's name 'Miss Heaven' on the package, and there's no answer after a few minutes. You jump back in the van and the second you switch the radio on, Bob Dylan sings 'Knock knock knocking on Heaven's door'. It was literally like that all day, every single song. Towards the end of my shift, I was approaching a roundabout when I couldn't take it anymore, in a funny way. I laughed and shouted aloud, 'If anyone is doing this to me, give me a sign!' As I stopped on that roundabout, there was a massive billboard that had massive writing that said 'Are you reading the signs?' and nothing else. Apologies for repeating, but I want it to sink into your brain that contact with the universe and its answers are right there in front of us. I asked the

Universe for a sign and it gave me a *literal* sign. This backs up my belief that as a human being, I'm currently only living as a fraction of myself and will return to my full, true self when I return 'up there'. The way my question was answered was funny and is definitely something 'up there' me would do because I'm actually rather hilarious.

Okay, fine, enough about me (for now). So, remember that ultimately, this is **your** reality. It's correct to say that we're all one, as we're all branches of the same tree, but think of *this* (right now) as your experience and your experience alone. Knowing this fact allows you to feel more at ease with contacting the knowledge 'up there'. You have a direct line 24/7. You are able to converse with the Universe about the smallest of manifestations. I've personally got to the point in my own life where I am now *subconsciously* speaking to the Source. A synchronicity can materialise in front of me whilst I'm mid-conversation with someone and I'll grin at the manifestation in autopilot because I work so closely with the Universe itself and 'up there' me. Step one is always to ask, step two is to believe and step three is to receive. It's mind-boggling when it starts happening for you, and I honestly can't wait for you to show up in my DMs (@coachbce on Twitter) and tell me how blown away you are.

Start right now by asking for a sign. Think of what it is that you really, truly, madly, deeply desire, create the feeling of joy and really embody that emotion when visualising the end result and ask the Universe for a sign to show that it's on its way. Then see.

Here's the process in more depth for you to follow:

Step One: Ask

This means two things: affirmations and asking for signs. I hope by now you've already started to write down your list of affirmations, so you've already 'asked', but also if you want a sign to appear in your life, you can also *verbally* ask the Universe for one. Always ask how you would ask a normal question to a friend and don't overcomplicate it. It shouldn't be a difficult task whatsoever.

A few months ago, I was a guest on the podcast *The Seed System* and we spoke about visualising cars. After the recording, I hopped back in the car and spoke to the Universe. I said 'Right, I want a Ferrari 360 Modena. Is that the right choice? Should I be manifesting a Ferrari right now? Can you please give me a sign through the radio?' Like I've previously stated, the Universe will communicate with you, and you'll receive your answers in the best way that *you* will understand, and one of the best ways for me is music. As I switched the radio on, the first lyrics were 'Ooh, you're moving too fast.' So then I responded with, 'Haha, okay, fair enough.' I couldn't quite figure out whether they were telling me to slow down and that I didn't need a supercar just yet, or if they were being funny and simply talking about the speed of the car itself!

It doesn't just have to be music, though! Remember when I told you to forget about the 'how'? Just ask the question and let the Universal Mind contact you in the way that it sees best. If your belief is strong enough, and I mean really strong, try it right now with this book. If you truly believe that you can speak with (not just *to*) the Universe, then ask it a question now and skip to a random page and read the first thing you see. Drop me a message if this works for you, and let me know what answer you received!

The key, though, is step two.

Step Two: Believe

Just like when we talked about the underlying emotions behind your affirmations, your belief that you *will* receive an answer to your question, or a sign or some synchronicities, is what'll cement the process and bring you your desired results. Once you've asked the question or asked for a sign, you have to then go about your day sincerely waiting for the answer. You don't need to necessarily look for the response, but if it's the first time that you've asked the Universe for something, you just need to be open to the possibility that the reply can come to you through any means. The Universe can reply through another human being too because after all, we're all extensions of the Source itself. One of your affirmations may be 'I'm a millionaire' and you might arrive at work the following day and the overly friendly regular customer will say, 'Wow, you look like a million dollars today.' Don't just be open to receiving the answer, have solid faith that it's already flying towards you, faster than the speed of light.

Step Three: Receive

This last step is the shortest and hopefully the easiest as it just relies on the previous steps having been done correctly. You ask, you fully believe and expect, and then you relax, kick back and simply allow your requests to be fulfilled.

***

I just want to take a moment here, before going any further, to tell you about the week I've just had. The past few days have been insane for me and a bunch of amazing manifestations have come true in my life. I'm only telling you this because there's a lesson or two I've learned that I want to teach.

The first thing is my most recent book, *Retired At 25: The Law of Attraction*, sold out on Amazon within the first week and is still rapidly continuing to climb the charts. My book is in the top 100, and even top 10, in several categories and I'm honestly blown away by the response.

What's made this week one of the best in my life, however, is finding out that we're having another baby!! Like I've previously stated, I've been manifesting a Lamborghini, simply because of all the steps I'll need to accomplish beforehand. Even though I *could* go out and buy one (and probably end up sleeping in the shed), there's a list of things I want to manifest first, so manifesting the current 'end goal', which is the Lambo, means that I would have already accomplished everything else first. Our plan is to have another baby, go travelling for at least a year, decide on a location to live, (probably) return back to the UK to buy a house and *then* buy the car. The baby is the first step on my list and obviously the biggest. I've always wanted a family, and even though I'm writing this as though our second baby is a 'step', I really do mean that it's the biggest, greatest manifestation I could possibly have created, along with my first child!

The lesson here, though, is about contradiction.

'THERE ARE NO PROBLEMS, ONLY SITUATIONS. IT IS ALL IN HOW YOU APPROACH THEM.'

—Sadhguru

CONTRADICTION

In this sense of the word, a contradiction is when your physical reality conflicts with your mental reality. I'm not just talking about when you're trying to manifest something that has yet to come true. I am talking about when you *prevent* your affirmations from coming true by contradicting them with your physical reality. Let's give an example.

Imagine that it's a Ferrari that you desire. You spend 30 minutes powerfully visualising yourself driving the car, maybe showing it off to family and friends or driving it to the beach. You add the elevated emotions that are required and truly feel as though the car is already yours, and not just on its way to you. You finish your visualisation session and open your eyes. You open your phone and go virtual car shopping online, searching for the car you're visualising, to strengthen the whole process. One of the first cars that you see is the exact colour, year, model, spec, has the same wheels and interior that you'd been visualising *and* it has your name or initials on the registration plate. This has happened to me many, many times. So, you've visualised well, felt the emotions, and the Universe has even shown you a synchronicity to tell you that your message has been received. But do you have room for the Ferrari? Could you park it in your street? Do you have a garage? The space? If not, the only thing stopping your desires reaching you is you.

Not everyone wants a Ferrari though, you're absolutely right. What about trying to manifest the perfect partner? Do you have space at home for them to live with you? Is there space in your wardrobe for their clothes? Do you have enough chairs at the dining table?

What about if you're trying to manifest pregnancy? Is there a spare room in your home? Do you have room for all the toys?

Now, let's link this to the manifestation of my partner's current pregnancy.

When you get seriously good at manifesting and creating your own reality, it gets harder *and* easier. It gets easier because you understand how it all works, can communicate with the Universe at will and can materialise anything you wish. It also gets harder because you overthink each manifestation and question each affirmation, which can lead to the creation of doubt. For example, when Jess became pregnant with our daughter, we had been trying (everything) for months and months. We'd also been 'not trying' but not stopping it from happening for around two years. Jess became pregnant the same week that I added 'Jess is pregnant' to my list of affirmations. This was easy because it was the first time I'd tried manifesting something like this. I had been manifesting cars and money with ease for a few months, so my mind was blown when I had this idea to write the pregnancy down as an affirmation. Now, though, because it *isn't* something new and fresh anymore, the second pregnancy didn't manifest in the same week that I wrote it down again. This was partly because I was overthinking the situation and the affirmation itself, but also because my physical reality was conflicting with and contradicting my mental reality. Like I said, our plan is to travel not long after the second baby arrives. I was constantly looking for villas and flights for the end of next year, hoping that we'd have another baby by then. But can you guess what I was doing wrong that was stopping the pregnancy from arriving? I was looking for places to stay abroad and flights to get there for two adults, *one* baby and two dogs. The realisation hit me, I changed my searches to *two* babies, and we had a positive pregnancy test in the same week.

How could the Universe have possibly delivered my desire if my brain didn't fully believe it? All the Universe could see was me wanting a baby, which is just a form of lack, because my physical actions were saying the opposite. Through my holiday searches, I was telling them and myself, actually, that I wasn't even expecting to have another child by next year.

Do you want to work in a professional position, like as a lawyer or financial advisor, for example? Buy a suit so that you're ready to start. Do you wish your dodgy knee was fully recovered? Then why do you keep that knee brace 'just in case'. You've really got to look into it *all* and include every aspect if you truly want to nail it and attract the biggest manifestations in the shortest time. If it is financial freedom that you desire, so you can spend all of your free time surfing or hiking, why are you slouching on the sofa in your spare time and partying every weekend? The Universe *knows* that you want to be able to spend all of your time at the beach or outdoors, but when you don't currently spend *any* free time doing just that, you contradict yourself.

This can be an eye-opener for a lot of people whilst on their conscious manifestation journeys, like it was for me. It can also teach you a lot about the way you really work, physically and mentally. To *really* get to know yourself, however, you should start writing.

‘WHEN WALKING, WALK. WHEN EATING, EAT.’
—Zen proverb

WRITE

This is the second book that I've written on this 'way of living', if you will, and you'd think that I would fully know myself before writing, especially when I'm trying to teach others how to get to know themselves, right? You'd be surprised. Writing this book has taught me *so* much about myself—it's crazy! This book has allowed me to call upon random past life experiences and then link them to a technique that I'm teaching, which makes them no longer random. I've recalled certain things that I'd thought were just subconscious moments of my life, only to find out that there actually *were* reasons behind the things that I've done. It's really like having a conversation with my own brain sometimes, which is why I'd recommend it. Before I give you suggestions though, here's a brief example.

When I was younger—I mean, when I'd orbited the sun less times than I currently have—I used to practice the Law of Attraction without even knowing. When I was in school, maybe around the age of say 14–17, whenever I'd wake up, I would tell myself that something amazing was literally around the corner and on its way to me. It gave me and my emotions something to look forward to, mentally. I have zero idea why I used to do this, and I literally must've just forgotten that I was doing it at one point and stopped. I only remembered that I used to do this because I was writing about it in this book. Once I remembered it, I realised that it had simply been a direct intervention from the Universe itself. Why on earth would I subconsciously, on autopilot, wake up and decide to think good thoughts? I wouldn't. However, like I've taught here in this book, you never truly forget what you knew *before* you came onto this plane. That mental morning routine that I'd had was just me 'up there' reconnecting with myself 'down here' to show me how reality *could* be once I realised I could take control of it. *That's* why I was always so happy growing up, because I constantly felt as though Christmas was right around the corner and I was going to open the best presents ever, metaphorically speaking. I would never have realised any of this if it wasn't for my own words in this book.

Obviously, I don't want you to write a book, even though you could. Just write to have a conversation with yourself. Think of yourself as being your own therapist for an hour. You can journal, write a small diary (daily, weekly or monthly), just write down your emotions or about certain situations and how you faced them—or even actually write a book. You can also write down your thoughts as you read this book and rediscover your true identity.

'AWAKENING IS NOT CHANGING WHO YOU ARE, BUT DISCARDING WHO YOU ARE NOT.'
—Deepak Chopra

ACTION

Your life can change drastically overnight, and I want to talk about both sides of that coin here. Once all of the lessons and techniques in this book begin to sink in and you start to implement them in your daily practices, you'll soon come to realise how the world *really* works. You'll understand, or actually *remember*, that the Universal field of consciousness, from which you came and to which you will return, has a never-ending stream of infinite knowledge that flows through you with every breath you take. You can harness this power at will, no matter what your desires are, just as long as you are following the correct steps. Once you really *do* see all of this and begin to see the effects unfold and your affirmations materialise in your own life, there is no 'wait' as such as to when you can manifest your visions. You can change your life (completely flip it, actually) overnight. I'm not just using this as a cliché term, either. This is a fact that I am living proof of. I went from having £200 to my name to making £45,000 per day at one point, all within the same year! My first manifestation was £1000, and that took less than five minutes of mental work each day for three days. That's £1000 for 15 minutes' work! I understand that neither of those examples happened *literally* overnight, but the mentality and outlook was. A flick of a switch, if you will.

The only reason that a vision will take a while to manifest is if you *believe* it is going to take a while, and that's it. If you truly know that you can draw your desires straight from the Source whenever you so wish, then nothing will get in the way of your masterpiece materialising. So the message here is that you *need* to know not only can you have it all but you can have it all now.

The other side of the coin reads the same, but with a different meaning. Yes, your life *can* completely change overnight, but sometimes not in the way you want it to. From my own personal experience, sometimes you just have no idea what's in store for you tomorrow. No matter how great you are at manifesting and creating each aspect of your reality, sometimes the Universe simply has other plans. Take my father, for example, 44 years old! In 18 years' time, I'll be older than my father, how crazy is that?! He was sitting downstairs in the early hours of one morning and just had a heart attack and died. End of story. My father had plans for tomorrow, the week later and the rest of his life, just like we all do. We all think death is just something that happens to someone else. I'm not trying to be morbid here and I'm almost not trying to pull on your heartstrings; I'm simply telling you that *today* is the day to start. Today is the first day of the rest of your life. No waiting until Monday, no telling yourself 'tomorrow', and no putting this book down to catch up on reality TV. I'm not even telling you to get up and do something external, just go within and use the techniques here in this book to your advantage and really start to take control.

I want to take another moment here, a pause from the book if you will. Is this an interval? Is this just me using this book as a personal diary to air my thoughts? It's been around a week for me since I told you here that my partner and I are expecting another baby. There's not a nice way to put it, but this week we were given the horrible news that we've had a miscarriage. It's shit, it is, but I wanted to tell you in this book. My first thought was to just delete the first paragraph where I told you, but I'm hoping you know by now how honest I am. It also goes to show that we're all (currently) human. I am confident enough to state that I can easily create my own reality, but sometimes life itself just has a slightly different plan.

Obviously, I've questioned a lot of things. How did I manifest the pregnancy and then it didn't work out? On a deeper level, I wondered whether I manifested it wrong. But you can't think like that. It's all part of the plan, I guess. The biggest message in me telling you this is that, besides manifesting and having a generally positive outlook, I want to be the perfect example to you that you *can* pull yourself out of whatever dark hole you find yourself in. If I can find my grandfather dead, almost lose my dog, go through my father dying suddenly at 44 and then lose a baby, and *still* hold my head high with a big fat smile on my face, you can pull through anything. It gets better when you do.

'EMOTIONS ARE LIKE PASSING STORMS, AND YOU HAVE TO REMIND YOURSELF THAT IT WON'T RAIN FOREVER.'

—Amy Poehler

PATIENCE

What's the rush? I know I've just spoken about how life can change (sometimes for the worse) literally overnight, so this section may be a contradiction. Anyway, the message here is that to really appreciate each moment that the Universe gifts us, we need to slow right down and have true patience. Throughout my life, I have always struggled with patience, or my lack of it. I always used to get really frustrated (never angry) really quickly, and usually over stupid things, too. For example, whenever Jess would take 40 minutes to get ready and I'd only take three, it'd infuriate me. Even if we were only going for a walk, I'd get so pissed off that we hadn't already left and that I was just waiting around. This was always the case, until I questioned it. *Why* was I getting so impatient just because I had to wait an extra few minutes, just to go somewhere that had no set time?

Are you also like this? Perhaps you've been in work, just about to close up shop for the night, and another customer comes in. Even though they'll only take one minute to grab one item, it affects you so much just because you have to do *nothing* for a few seconds. Think about a time when you were at an airport and waiting for your flight. There are a few hundred of you waiting for the flight attendants to come out, take your passports and allow you to board the plane. Even though you are all literally just waiting to go and sit somewhere else and then do even *more* waiting, there's a collective impatience amongst the group, for no reason whatsoever.

In many people, actually, it comes down to control. When a person is 'waiting' for something or someone and the length of waiting has no true bearing on their life, but they still become impatient, they are frustrated that they are no longer in control. They aren't physically doing anything and just want to be 'on the move', where they can take back control as they move forward. You'll learn to find peace when you realise that all you need to control is yourself, internally.

Once I questioned why I was really always getting frustrated, I had no actual answer. I just needed to relax. An extra few minutes of waiting had no true bearing on the day, whatsoever. I then decided that I'd use that spare time to read, to learn, to ground myself, to focus on my breathing, to visualise, to sing, to dance. How often do you get to the end of the night and think 'Ah, I *did* want to read a few pages of that new book tonight,' but not had the 'time'? You've always had the time! You've just wasted it by wishing it was over.

Some people are genuinely, and unbeknownst to them, scared of spending time with themselves. Just being on their own for a few minutes allows them to be *alone* with their thoughts, which they believe isn't necessarily a good thing. If someone is angry with their life or is going through a rough patch and then has to wait for their partner to get ready, for example, they can get frustrated because they aren't physically and, more importantly, mentally busy. This lack of activity means that they ponder and revisit scenarios in their head that they aren't happy with, and all they can do in response to that is blurt out 'Hurry up!' on autopilot.

You need to understand that you can replace a lack of patience with being present in the moment. Think of how much time you waste while being impatient for something. Whether it's a certain day, a bus or even your computer has frozen, appreciate the 'waiting time' that you'd usually wish away, using the appreciation techniques that you've learned.

'YOU'LL BE CALM THE DAY YOU LEARN TO SIT ALONE AND DO NOTHING.'

—Maxime Lagace

LIMITS

If this isn't your first mindset book, you'll have heard the concept of 'limiting beliefs'. It's rather obvious what they are, but let's go in depth so we can tear them apart and create new beliefs.

Limiting beliefs apply everywhere, in every aspect of our lives, and can be created by ourselves or given to us by others. For example, one of mine was that I'd never be 'big' enough when I started lifting weights. My mother had always told me that I'd never be big because I 'wasn't built like that'. This stuck in my head and became a limiting belief, meaning that whenever I felt as though I was too skinny, that belief would echo in my head and reassure my ego that I couldn't get big because I wasn't built that way. Another was when I became a personal trainer and one guy told me I couldn't be one and wouldn't be successful because I didn't have a qualification in nutrition. Whenever I'd have a client who didn't get on with a certain diet I'd given them, the guy's words would play on my mind and make me doubt myself in that career.

Many limiting beliefs are so deep within and started at such a young age that we don't even know they're there. For example, when you were a child, can you recall your parents saying that 'money doesn't grow on trees' and 'we aren't made of money'? Did they set the tone that money was something that you simply couldn't acquire unless you were born into it or had a stupidly well-paying job? This kind of belief is a consistent one, meaning that it was repeatedly ingrained into your brain as you grew up, so much so that you took it as a second language and believed in it more than believing the sea is blue.

Can you think of examples from your own life? If not, dig deeper. Try and write down three of your own limiting beliefs and try to identify the source of each idea and who gave it to you. It may be related to work, your physical health or even your financial status. Unfortunately, it's usually passed down to us by our parents, but that's through no fault of their own, as it was merely passed down to them also. Think about it. If your father always told you that money was hard to come by and that no matter how hard you worked, you'd always be scraping by, where did that limiting belief come from? This is a bit of a 'down the rabbit hole' answer, but here goes: this limiting belief can come from a hand-me-down limiting belief *and* life experience. But the life experience that gives you the impression that 'money is hard to come by' is only so because you've created it that way and manifested it by *believing* in the limiting belief that your parents gifted you. Does that make sense? If your father believed in that limiting belief that his father gave to him, he'd ultimately create his own reality around that belief, thus reinforcing it and allowing him to pass it on to you. This goes on for generations, until one child takes a step back and questions it. That's how you end it. That's how you break the curse.

Like a lot of answers in this book, you need to question the belief to find the source. You need to follow the branch until you get to the root. Ask yourself *why* you have that particular limiting belief, *who* gave it to you (if anyone did) and what do you now *want* to believe? Just like you learned this false belief about yourself, you can unlearn it. As you should know by now, you have the power to choose your own thoughts and feel whatever emotions you want to feel. Now you can begin to understand that you can believe *whatever* belief you want about yourself. Were you always told you'd work a minimum wage job for your entire life? Fuck that and fuck the person that told you. It is time to set unlimited beliefs for yourself. It is time to rewire your brain for the better, mentally create the new you and then physically embody it. You can do this with your affirmations, too, if you'd like. Try adding an opinion about yourself that you'd love to be true, and believe it. Do you play football yet never score a goal, and that ties in with one of your limiting beliefs? Add the affirmation 'I score at least one goal in every match' or 'I'm the best football player in my area'. Do this and watch how your opinion of yourself and even your confidence changes. Do not be unhappy by settling for something that you can change.

To sum up the whole idea of limiting beliefs, take Roger Bannister. Bannister ran track back in the '50s and he ran a mile in 3 minutes and 59.4 seconds. He broke the world record when he did this in 1954 because no one had ever managed to run a mile in under four minutes. As a matter of fact, it was deemed 'impossible' for a human. Not a single athlete was able to beat the four-minute mark before Bannister, solely due to the fact that they all had the same limiting belief that it was impossible. It took 46 days for his record to be beaten, and since that day in '54, over 1400 athletes have run a mile in under four minutes! First, you have to break the mental barrier, *then* the physical one.

'FAITH AND FEAR BOTH DEMAND YOU BELIEVE IN SOMETHING YOU CANNOT SEE. YOU CHOOSE.'

—Bob Proctor

STORY

I've got this section in my head but feel as though it'll be a challenge to put it into words. It will use a lot of the ideas from the other sections combined. So, without further ado, what's *your* story? When someone asks you about yourself, your life, your upbringing, your skills, your insecurities, what do you say? Probably, 'Mind ya business, ya nosey creep.' But the answers that you *do* have, you know you can alter those, right? A common phrase that's used by many is 'the next chapter of my life'. What's obvious about that phrase? The person speaking it believes that their life is a story. If this is true, and our lives *are* stories, metaphorically speaking, then who's the author? Is it our parents? Our teachers? Our boss? God?

Nope, us. *We* are the authors. *You* are the author of your own life story. I know that it sounds like a big fat cliché, but it's the only truth you'll ever need to know. Really let it sink in that only you are able to write your own life story.

Okay, now that you know that's a fact, why are you writing such a shit life? No offence. There isn't a way to put it without being blunt. There's a very big chance that you've picked up a copy of this book (thank you, again) because you want to make your life better. Is that true for you? But now you've come to realise that you've been writing your own story that you hate so much! The way that you've written your story so far has been influenced by a bunch of stuff I've already mentioned in this book. For example, let's say that you hate your job. There can be an infinite number of reasons for this, and each reason may potentially have stemmed from another reason. What do I mean by this? So, you may hate your job simply because you believe it's an awful job, and that's okay. But where did that idea come from? Here are a few options using previous sections of this book, just so you can see how they are all applicable to a vast amount of areas in your life:

- The media has drilled into your brain that you need a better-paying job to have more money so you can be deemed successful.
- Your ego wants you to be perceived as 'above' your peers and everyone else on the financial and status ladder.
- Your parents have always told you that this is just the way the world (and corrupt government) works and you *must* work a shit job for 40+ years, just to get a shit pension.
- You may have a limiting belief given to you by a parent, teacher or boss that makes you feel as though you aren't *worthy* of a better job.
- You're living on autopilot, meaning that even though you hate your job, you aren't living consciously enough to decide to do something to change it.
- You don't appreciate the job by looking for the positive aspects and the fact that your wage keeps a roof over your head.

Or it could be a combination of these:

- Your parents' limiting beliefs about it being necessary to work a job you hate, just to get by, subconsciously caused you to seek out a 'bad' job when you were looking for one. You started the job with the belief that it would be a job that you hated, and thus you partner up with the Universe to make it so. Your mental affirmations that you repeat to your subconscious mind whilst in autopilot include 'I hate this job', and as you continuously repeat that to yourself, you manifest it in your physical reality. As soon as you start picking out the negative things in that job and branding it as 'shit', your ego is at ease because all of your beliefs have come true.

Do you now see how it all links? You have designed it all.

Your life is a video game that you have developed and coded the exact way that it is, which is subconsciously to your own preference!

'WHAT OTHERS THINK ABOUT YOU IS NONE OF YOUR BUSINESS.'

—Jack Canfield

FACETIME

Maybe this section is a little 'off-topic', but I guess I'm just adding sections to this book when they appear in my mind. The question that I want to pose is this: what the fuck have we all become? Our phones have become more than a part of our lives; they've taken over. Are we cyborgs? What happens when our mobile devices are just about to run out of battery whilst we're using them? We pop the charger in and find ourselves in a ball-and-chain situation where we're confined to one meter away from the plug socket. In these moments, we are well and truly 'plugged in'.

Don't get it twisted, though: technology can be great. After all, it's the future, isn't it? What I will say is don't let it change you, just allow it to *benefit* you. Use it and make sure that *it* isn't using you. Let me dive into an example.

You have a holiday booked to your favourite destination, a week in the sun. You get there and as soon as you are able to, even before you fully unpack your suitcase, you're at the pool and relaxing on a lounger. What's missing from the picture here? Oh, of course, your mobile phone! It's not really missing though, is it? It's in your hand! You're posting photos on Facebook and adding to your Instagram story. On a deeper level, briefly, this is solely down to your ego and it wanting to look better than everyone else. The typical accompanying caption is 'I've had worse Mondays'.

This is your ego creating the false reality that you're basically retired for the week, allowing your internet friends and followers to feel envious and depressed because you've attacked their egos. Okay, that's enough 'deeper level' for this section. Now for reality.

If you're on holiday and are spending the same amount of time on your phone as you usually do at home, then you are effectively spending hundreds or even thousands just to be absorbed by your mobile in a different location. How bizarre is that, when you really think about it?

This chapter is knowledge and insight directly from personal experience. A few years ago, Jess and I spent a little over two weeks in Phuket, Thailand, and we thoroughly enjoyed it. But I would've enjoyed it a lot more if I wasn't constantly on the lookout for 'photo opportunities' for my social media accounts. I have no real idea as to why I was doing it, either! Other than the fact that I was on autopilot and brainwashed into the idea that we all *must* broadcast our lives (the good parts, anyway) on social media, merely to show our life progress and successes. I just wanted to keep up my 'social presence', I guess, but I was barely getting ten likes per post! It doesn't make sense, but we've all been victims of it.

I even tried to optimise views and likes. I'd figure out the time back home in the UK and then plan when I would post my photos. My thought process was something along the lines of, *'Well, if I post one photo at 8 a.m. and one at 6 p.m. UK time, people back home will see my photos just before they go to work and when they come home.'* I'd even post photos a day or two after we'd arrive back home to act like I was still there, making people jealous that I could afford such a long holiday! It's like having an ego disease, and it, unfortunately, consumes many of us in a number of ways.

It's becoming increasingly difficult to put our phones down, and obviously, it's cleverly designed that way to keep our attention a prisoner to our devices. Today, it isn't as easy as putting our phones down and leaving them down, because we depend on them so much. You could decide to have a social media detox, but then what about work emails? Internet banking? Taking photos? Productive apps? Learning apps? Navigation? Google?

As I write this chapter, I'm in a lodge on day three of our holiday. We are almost in the middle of nowhere and right on the edge of a cliff, overlooking the sea. It actually sounds rather dangerous now that I'm writing it down, but hey ho. Why am I telling you this? Because I don't have my phone with me! I'm even writing this with pen and paper. Old school as fuck! We're also pregnant again! Don't tell anyone!

Being without your phone is more than possible, we've just conditioned (or have been conditioned to condition) our subconscious minds into believing that we *need* our phones and that they are but extensions of ourselves. Here's a hard pill to swallow: they aren't! You cannot truly live in and appreciate each moment with your phone on your person. Your inner belief system *wants* you to be distracted. Actually, that's another good point: the root of the distraction.

I've been there, two hours deep into Instagram Reels, an hour deep into Spider-Man memes and an hour deep into car review videos. But why? What's the point? No, really, what *is* the actual point? Does it really benefit us? Of course not. Is it just a prolonged dopamine hit? It does cure our boredom though, right? Or are we just subconsciously filling a void that we didn't even know of?

Oh great, here he goes again with 'subconscious'. Don't you own a thesaurus, Ben?

If you're spending hours upon hours every single night mindlessly scrolling through your apps or playing video games, what are you avoiding? We've talked about how powerful it can be to pause, take a step back and question ourselves, our thoughts and our actions. So the next time you find yourself 'curing your boredom', ask yourself if there's anything you're avoiding. It could be a variety of things, including the avoidance of:

- Cleaning the house
- Contacting a certain person
- Thinking about a recent breakup
- Grief
- Trauma
- Self-doubt about your career
- Unhappiness or stagnation in life
- Or many other things!

It may just be a case of 'Well, Ben, I've got fuck-all else to do, so let me play FIFA in peace!', but simply curing boredom is rarely the case once you peek below the surface.

'WHETHER YOU THINK YOU CAN, OR YOU THINK YOU CAN'T, YOU'RE RIGHT.'

—Henry Ford

LOVE

Ego. I know that by now you have come to realise that it plays, or used to play, a massive role in your emotions and many of your daily activities. I want to briefly touch upon something else that also flows through all of our actions. Love.

Let's ponder the meaning of those four letters. What if love is all life is truly about? Are we just here on Earth and in this life to *experience* love in all its glory? To give love? Receive love? Is love just another word for life itself? My favourite film of all time, *Interstellar*, puts it best:

'Maybe [love] means something more—something we can't yet understand. Maybe it's some evidence, some artefact of a higher dimension that we can't consciously perceive. I'm drawn across the universe to someone I haven't seen in a decade who I know is probably dead. Love is the one thing that we're capable of perceiving that transcends dimensions of time and space. Maybe we should trust that, even if we can't understand it.'

I've come to realise that all we really remember about our loved ones who have passed away is how much or how little they loved us. We also remember our love for them, otherwise we wouldn't miss them, right? Of course, we remember the good things and we also remember the bad, but aren't those memories just examples of showing/not showing love? It goes further than people we've lost, too. Think of someone that you dislike or maybe someone who wasn't particularly nice to you in school. What is it about them that you don't/didn't like? Whatever reason you come up with, the underlying cause is their lack of love toward you, if you really think about it. That's my two cents on love, I guess.

'IF YOU WANT TO FIND THE SECRETS OF THE UNIVERSE, THINK IN TERMS OF ENERGY, FREQUENCY AND VIBRATION.'

—Nikola Tesla

GO

You are now ready; you now hold the key (or keys?). I sincerely hope that the words I have written on these pages excite you and motivate you to make a difference in your life the second that you put this book down. Just do *one* thing! That's all it takes. Write down some affirmations, visualise, question your ego, understand the thought processes of your family members to see *why* they do what they do. One simple step is all that it takes to propel you to the future that you so desire and, more importantly, deserve. If you find yourself in a rut or what you feel is a dark place, I hope that my own life experience shows you that everything is a lesson and that the true answers are already within you, waiting to be found. If you are in a dark place, though, and you're able to think a single positive thought (imagining yourself on a private island, soaking up the sun, for example) and can put yourself in a mental position where your thoughts are 51% positive and 49% negative, then you've already tipped the scales in your favour. That's all it takes to begin: one great, joy-provoking thought and vision.

What do you really want out of life? Is that a question that you've *really* thought about? As I've said, our sole purpose here on Earth is to seek and spread joy. Do your life goals allow both of those things to happen? Ask yourself right now what the 'end goal' is for you. Where are you five years from now? Where are you next year? I've explained just how quick your life can change, so start acting like it.

Let's imagine that you're handed a bank card with an abundance of money on it, no strings attached. All your bills are automatically paid each month and you've just bought every single thing you could possibly wish for. What now? What are you going to be doing each and every day? Whatever your answer may be, keep *that* as the vision. Imagine yourself starting up your boat, ready to take your family on the water for a few hours, not a care in the world. Later on in the day, you'll take your supercar for a spin around the mountains and then return to your family to appreciate the evening with your loved ones. That's the vision for most people, and all you need to do for it to come true is to keep that vision/thought/affirmation as your sole intention. It'll manifest before you know it.

Smash it,
Ben Cole-Edwards

AUTHOR PROFILE

Ben Cole-Edwards is a mindset expert and certified Life Coach. One of Ben's major aims in life is to spread his knowledge regarding the Law of Attraction, Manifesting and Affirmations to everyone he can, allowing others to find their own happiness and achieve everything they've ever desired.

Twitter: @coachbce

WHAT DID YOU THINK OF F*CK YOUR EGO?

A big thank you for purchasing this book. It means a lot that you chose this book specifically from such a wide range on offer. I do hope you enjoyed it.

Book reviews are incredibly important for an author. All feedback helps them improve their writing for future projects and for developing this edition. If you are able to spare a few minutes to post a review on Amazon, that would be much appreciated.

PUBLISHER INFORMATION

Rowanvale Books provides publishing services to independent authors, writers and poets all over the globe. We deliver a personal, honest and efficient service that allows authors to see their work published, while remaining in control of the process and retaining their creativity. By making publishing services available to authors in a cost-effective and ethical way, we at Rowanvale Books hope to ensure that the local, national and international community benefits from a steady stream of good quality literature.

For more information about us, our authors or our publications, please get in touch.

www.rowanvalebooks.com
info@rowanvalebooks.com

Printed in Great Britain
by Amazon